STRAIGHT OUTTA COMPTON

Straight Outta Compton

Ricardo Cortez Cruz

A dive into living large,

a work where characters trip,

talk out the side of their neck

and cuss like it was nothing.

FICTION COLLECTIVE TWO

Normal • Boulder

This book is the winner of the 1991 Charles H. and N. Mildred
Nilon Excellence in Minority Fiction Award, sponsored by the
University of Colorado and Fiction Collective Two

Published jointly by the University of Colorado and Fiction
Collective Two with assistance from the National Endowment
for the Arts and the support of the Publications Center of the
University of Colorado at Boulder and Illinois State University,
English Department Publications Unit

Address all inquiries to: Fiction Collective Two, c/o Publications
Center, University of Colorado, Boulder, CO 80309-0226

Straight Outta Compton
Ricardo Cortez Cruz

ISBN: Cloth, 0-932511-60-0
ISBN: Paper, 0-932511-61-9

Manufactured in the United States of America
Distributed by the Talman Company

To my family, inc., Greg & Rodney

"We can think of composition as 'a bundle of parts'."

—Ann Berthoff, *The Making of Meaning*

The Metropolis

*Once upon a time in a land called a metropolis
where little boys expressed their feelings in one
particular way, shooting the pill.*

*Where little boys put on their Air Jordans and
played the game of the neighborhood,
basketball.*

*The little boys couldn't always play, because
the evil gangbangers took their Wilson
basketball.*

*But the little boys always got over, because they
had a goal in life, and that goal was to get out
of the ghetto and they did.*

—Jose Chambers,
"fresh" composition,
used with permission

Tomorrow

WHEN ROOSTER WAS
nine or so, we used to all sit on the stoop with boodies like
charcoal and scratch house music on the cement. Our mommas
were Lisa-Lisa and Monet grabbing Bic pens and No. 2 pencils
which were snapped in half. They threw them out the front door
and told us to get outside and use them. "Reclaim your imagination," momma said. "Keep your ass out of the street and put on
clean underwear in case you get hit."

Out on the stoop, I called Clive. And Clive called Rooster. And
Rooster would call nobody but talk only to himself. But Billy heard
Rooster clean down the end of the street, and he blew his plastic
bugle until his cheeks and heart turned blue. And he called
Yolanda. And Yolanda, who had squash for breasts, called dirty
Diana. And dirty Diana would drop her clothes and creep over
with ripe raspberries inside her unbuttoned blouse. And Rooster
would look inside and point at the berries like they were nothing.
And Clayborn would crawl alongside Diana and a cloud of dusties
so his momma and daddy couldn't see him, and he called nobody
but seemed to be calling for anybody on the inside. And anybody
who heard him called their friends and came over, and house
niggers who weren't even invited to sit on the stoop gave Flip,
Billy's tripped-out friend, an excuse to follow suit. So he did. And

Flip looked like a middle finger to us, but together we functioned like a bad set of big, black hands.

The University of Compton was close to my house, and Flip claimed he jumped the fence to become a college man. He pointed to the chain nets on the basketball courts inside the fence and showed us real blood smeared over his wrist and hand. Flip claimed he cut himself dunking on the rims. He also said it was where the drug dealers shoot.

While Flip was talking, Rooster repeated everything he heard: "Real blood. Real weapons. Real death."

Flip stopped and popped Rooster on the head. "What's your trip?" he asked.

The air was gray and full of cement, the smog revealing nothing in the sky but distant freeways and concrete buildings.

"That's heavy stuff," Clive said.

When Flip heard the word "stuff," he pointed to the court and claimed that there was pieces of thin rusty chain all over the ground.

"They don't make chains anymore the way they used to," I said. I scribbled some funky words on paper, wrote a piece of hype about the chains being dope and Flip bleeding, hopefully, HIV-negative.

"With this book, I'll make a fortune."

Flip was dripping, but it didn't seem to faze him. He kept talking smack, his story getting more and more depressing with each lie. Clive and Rooster kept handing me blue pens and stupid pencils that wouldn't write.

The more interesting story was Yolanda reading *The Dutchman* and cussing, screaming that whoever became her man better not let her catch him fucking a white woman. She was a mulatto and, consequently, she was blessed with good hair and relationships that usually turned out bad.

Perhaps sensing when a woman was down, Rooster would find and pick on Yolanda when he was bored or upset. Clive would be holding Rooster's bare stomach and unwrapping Bazooka bubble gum, reading his fortune. Bosco asked for the wrappers, to read the comics, and Rooster snatched the gum and chewed it. Rooster loved sugar. He chomped on the gum like it was nothing. Large pieces of Bazooka exploded in his mouth until he threw the wad away.

"You want a piece, Miss Thang?" Rooster asked Yolanda. He didn't know what he was saying.

"Shut up, Rooster," said Billy. He sort of liked Rooster.

"He didn't mean it," said Clive. Clive was like a big brother to Rooster, whose real daddy ran away from him when he was very little.

"So," said Billy. "He was staring at Yolanda's boody."

Billy picked up two bundles of old newspapers—the *Los Angeles Times* and *LA Sentinel*—raised them over his big head and then hurled them at us, gray pages flying everywhere.

Billy whipped out his plastic bugle and blew on it. "Attention," he shouted. "From this day on, I decree Rooster to be the enemy. So let it be written, so let it be done."

"You big Ten Commandments head," I yelled to Billy.

"Shut up, gawddammit!" Billy yelled.

"Leave Billy alone!" Yolanda screamed. She sat next to Diana, who was squeezing juice from her blouse and smiling at Rooster and Clive.

"What's she grinning about?" Flip asked. He didn't like Clive-nem getting all of the attention.

"Who?" I asked.

Flip pointed his finger in Diana's face.

"Don't be an asshole!" Clive shouted. Bosco cracked up.

"What you laughing at?" Flip asked.

"Be cool," I told Flip, fingering me behind my back.

"Why don't you ask Billy Bugle Boy to be your boyfriend?" said Flip. He wanted cheap thrills.

"I will," said Yolanda. She wanted a man.

"When?" Flip asked. He'd break his neck and stop on a dime to see Yolanda sleep with someone.

"Billy, will you go with me?" she asked.

Everyone got quiet. Billy nodded his big head in approval. He wanted to be the first to get it.

Yolanda wheeled back around and cheesed, playing the nutroll. "There," she said. It was a done deal.

"You act like a whore," Clive said.

Rooster repeated the line.

"Well, I'm not!" Yolanda insisted.

"Be quiet!" Flip shouted to Clive. "That's Billy's girl you talking about."

"So?" said Clive.

"Cool out," I told Clive.

"Cool out," said Rooster.

Billy faked like he was going to hit Rooster in the mouth.

Yolanda jumped up. "The next time he opens his big mouth I'm gonna hit him myself," she said.

"What's your problem?" Clive asked.

"Yeah, what's yo' problem?" Rooster asked.

"He's gonna have to show me respect," Yolanda said. Rooster picked up a water gun and shot her.

Bosco broke out laughing. "Rooster got you good," Bosco said.

"He should have squirted you in the mouth," said Flip.

Yolanda marched over and snatched the gun out of Rooster's hand. "You couldn't hurt a fly with that," she said.

"If he wanted to do some good, he ought to hit dirty Diana with some water," Flip said.

"Why you say that?" Clive asked.

"She stinks," Flip replied.

"Please," said Carlos. He was dressing a Black Barbie Doll with a swimsuit.

"Shut up, you faggot!" Flip yelled.

"Shut up," said Rooster.

Flip looked at Diana, whose berries were smashed and hurtin', and pointed his finger in her face. "If you don't believe me, smell her!"

"Smell her yourself!" Clive shouted.

Flip covered his ears. "Your mouth is bigger than Aretha Franklin's!" he said.

"Chee, chee." Carlos was giggling his big head off. He fell to the ground, weeds all in his hair.

"You guys have a problem!" Yolanda screamed.

"I'm not in it," I said.

"Me either," said Clive.

"Leave me out of it," I said.

Clive said "peace out" and did the new and improved two snaps and a circle.

"C'mere, sweet thang," said Rooster. "Come to daddy."

"Why is he talking to her like that?" Yolanda asked.

"He doesn't know what he's saying," Clive said.

"Where does he get it from?" Yolanda asked, multi-colored African beads from her necklace going shake-shake-shake around her neck.

"He repeats what he hears," Clive answered.

"Very touching," said Flip. "Tell him if he wants that little thang, he can have her."

"She's not your thang!" Yolanda shouted.

"That's because I gave it to Rooster," Flip said.

"You got a dirty mind," said Clive.

"Dirty mind," Rooster said.

"What's your trip?" Flip asked Rooster on the stoop, the only place where one's shit got checked publicly. "Who are you? The head Negro?"

Bosco busted out, wiping his forehead.

"It ain't funny," Flip said. Flip pointed at Clayborn sitting by himself. He was inventing a way to program ghettoized suicidal tendencies—the patent pending.

"I want to be a computer," Clayborn muttered. His only brother had jumped off the Colorado Bridge in Pasadena and killed himself. They found blood down by the Rose Bowl.

"I want to be a doctor!" Bosco shouted.

"You can't be a doctor, you Black motherfucker!" Flip yelled for no reason.

"Black motherfucker," Rooster repeated.

Down the street, past a line of laundry on wooden clothespins, Clive's daddy was hiding underneath somebody's porch and snorting white bricks, gold rubber hoses all up in his nose. We saw his big head peek out from the ground to see who was cussing. "Shut the fuck up," Clive's daddy shouted. He sent Clive a coke stare.

"Yo' daddy is livin' large," Billy said.

"God made him funky," Flip said.

Yolanda and Diana turned cartwheels like it was none of their business. Their heads looked like hanging pots.

"Your mother goes to sleep funky," Clive told Flip. "At least my daddy ain't selling it."

"You guys are a trip," I said. "Chill out."

"I know you're not talking to me," Yolanda said.

"This is my house!" I yelled. "Get the fuck out of here!"

"Hate you," said Rooster. He shot Billy in the butt with water.

"You a motherfucking trip," Rooster told Billy.

"Come on, let's go," Flip said. "We all can't in the same gang."

"Good riddance," I said.

They did a cock-of-the-walk stride and moved the crowd, dirty Diana looking behind and grinning at Clive and Rooster.

After Flip, Billy, Diana and Yolanda left, Clive-nem felt my forehead, waiting for a logical explanation as to why I suddenly went off.

"What are you all looking at?" I asked, staring Clive straight in the face. "Fuck off."

I get tired of people questioning everything I do, so I got up and went inside the house, ego-tripping. Clive-nem strolled down the street where a crowd of Black people was dramatizing Gwendolyn Brooks' poem "We Real Cool" and filming it. It was as if Compton was the mecca for Blacks, another fatherless Black producer trying to create a blockbuster movie out of the ghetto.

"Sayonara," I said.

When I stepped into the kitchen, Momma checked me immediately.

"Sit your little ass down at the table," she said. She played gospel music on compact disc, The Winans singing "your tomorrow could very well begin today." In the living room, somebody was playing Public Enemy singing "Don't Believe The Hype."

Momma banged pots and pans while holding Arm & Hammer and fussing. Daddy lay in the only bedroom like he didn't care, his brown caked hands folded up behind his big head. Momma got black-eyed peas and reheated them as leftovers, Daddy shouting for her to shut up unless she wanted them to duke it out again.

My brother and sister rushed out of the living room where they were sleeping and sat down at the table. We ate black-eyed peas like they were nothing. My sister kept trying to fill her plastic bowl to the top, so I pushed her in the face and she dropped her beans all over the yellow tile on the floor. Momma was pissed.

"You need to take your ass to bed," she said.

"I am," I said. Then I turned my back on her. "I didn't want beans anyway."

"Beans, beans, good for the heart—the more you eat, the more you fart!" my sister yelled.

I threw her doll on the floor, marched into the bedroom and fell out. When I looked out the bedroom window, Rooster and them were still out in the street, Clive playing tug-of-war with his daddy by the porch. Clive's daddy was shooting gravy up his arm like it was water. He had taken the rubber hoses out of his nose in order to wrap them around his arm. They looked like snakes biting his skin.

"Stop it!" I heard Clive's momma shout.

Clive's daddy shoved a group of people away from him, sprinkling sugar on the pavement as if it were bitter salt. Niggers backed up and watched, some afraid that this man was the devil or that he would try to kill them, the whole nine.

Clive's daddy hollered and spat blood on the sidewalk. He went off, a Medusa turning shell-shocked niggaz into stone.

"Poison!" he shouted, drug dealers standing there tripping and eating sweets, Funfetti dropping out of their mouths.

Clive's daddy started dripping malaria. It was if his body had been sucked dry. He was funky cold.

Just like that, he fell out, the *LA Sentinel* running away from him in the breeze shouting Sunday's news.

While niggaz shot pool on the corner, the *LA Sentinel* took off towards Heaven, word up.

Momma's Game

M Y MAN FLIP IS A TRIP.
Take last night, for example: Flip played himself...
He was talking rhetoric. Talking trash. Throwing hype. Shootin'
off his fat lip. Running off at the mouth. Pitching a hitch. Hitting
us with all kinds of yacky-yack/mucty-muck. Singing honky-tonk
tunes telling our big heads to hit the road, Jack. Gum-beating.
Going for soul. Giving out. But not giving a shit. Not giving us five.
Not giving the drummer some. Freezing his homeboys into rock
candy, while he was eatin' it up. Blowing his gut. Cracking up.
Absofuckinglutely. Squalling as we sat on the stoop looking stupid
out in the middle of a storm on Seventh Avenue in Harlem, during
Daddy-week of all times, rain pellets wopping our big heads like
cough drops. Like rocks. Like Staley syrup boiled in a tin sauce-
pan.

Flip kept on talking that drag while we watched Willie sell sugar
on the edge of the corner.

(Thangs you put up with in Soul City when you're not stinkypie
rich or wailing at the Apollo Theatre or watching a livingroom gig
on the sunny side of the street is what Flip reminded us of.)

"Go-man-go!" we shouted to Flip.

(Thangs you intentionally say in order to give someone the big
head.)

I closed my eyes and *let the rain do me up.* We used to play football in the rain. *The brown ball would be soaked and lopsided, but I was able to throw it about 30 yards down the field.*

Flip fell for it, taking it all in and pointing to the threads he had on as if he was clean/fonky/mod/ragged/sharp/silked and tabbed to the bone.

"You a caution sign," Clive hollered to Flip, breaking up.

Flip had on brown leather Hush Puppies, pink socks, potato-sack pants, a metallic belt, a plaid shirt, an ugly beige fish tie, a fuchsia pocket silk and a red, white and black bandanna around his nappy head.

Sometimes it would be cold and the ball would be wet, so we'd have to wipe our hands on our sleeves or handkerchiefs. My fingers felt numb and slippery, but I was still able to throw the football about 30 yards in a tight spiral. Flip dove for the ball and wrapped it up tightly in his arms, looking down at himself as he slid along the fence.

"You think I'm cute?" he asked. He was holding up a hand mirror.

We paused and waited for a stray dog to quit howling before we answered his question.

"We refuse to talk," said Rooster.

Rooster covered me up and then did the rumba to keep warm. My fingers felt like hard sticks of Wrigley's spearmint gum in the cold, and, even underneath the quilt, I could still see my breath linger in the air. I blew some more into the air and sighed.

After waving the mirror in front of his face, Flip dropped it and then looked disgusted: "Quit playing," he said.

Flip looked funny because he was dark skin, and he appeared to have mud or Oil of Olay or something on his face. He had five stitches inside his mouth from fighting, and his pinkie was dislocated.

This may sound crazy, but every now and then Flip reminds me of myself. My Momma used to say that I played too rough around my sister. I used to practice falling down the steps so I could scare my family and make them think that I was hurt. I don't do that sort of stuff anymore. Now I sit and watch Momma. Momma's got barb wires on top of her big head and calluses on her feet. She says that I am always in her way while she is trying to cook in the kitchen. When Momma says things like that she bothers me, but I don't say anything.

"*We refuse to talk,*" *Rooster reiterated.*

"Suit yourself," said Flip. He was a conceited devil. And now, he was clutching a bottle of Mad Dog and taking swigs like it was nothing.

"Bust my booty," Flip whispered to Rooster, cackling.

Flip looked like a drunk driving home on the freeway as he ran on the brown grass and mud while holding the pigskin, his shoelaces bobbing up and down. He weaved in and out of would-be tacklers by sheer luck. If he had the sense to know how to run, he probably would have gotten decked in a matter of seconds. But because everyone could tell that Flip didn't know what he was doing, they hesitated to come close to him. With Flip acting so crazy out on the field in the cold weather, laying a finger on him was like hitting Stonehenge with your bare hand. Robert Dorsey said he cried at the thought of having to bring him down. Flip told Robert off. He said that Robert had "too much blubber" to catch up to him anyway. Robert looked real funny, and then he started crying.

"*Book it,*" *said Flip.*

He was talking out the side of his neck because he had been drinking seemingly a toilet-full of panther piss. He went to Super Liquor and got it. In my neighborhood, the only identification you need is money. It doesn't take that many bills to get panther piss, though. Panther piss is this funky, yellowish cheap booze that is so nasty it makes you want to puke. Only a dog would drink it. These suckers must imagine it to be some sort of health tonic. After all, Flip be swallowing it as if water, wine, high fructose corn syrup, natural flavors, citric acid, sodium benzoate and sulphur dioxide were nutritious chemicals that could make him feel good, make him trip/ill/play the nutroll.

"How come this howling dog keeps pawing me in my stomach?" Flip asked. "It's makin' me feel awfully funny."

The dog began jumping up and down and crossways as if it were performing Stupid Pet Tricks for the David Letterman show; it almost knocked Flip down to the dirt.

"Get off me!" Flip demanded. "You makin' me sick."

The dog barked as it threw its sex organs up against Flip's leg in order to get its fore-paws planted higher on his soft belly.

Twisting its big head to an angle, the dog looked up at Flip like Lassie or Benji or Ben or one of those false-endearing animals that would do anything for a biscuit or a cool drink.

"Give it up," the dog said.

Man, did Flip's face turn red. He grabbed his Louisville slugger off the ground and tried to ice the mutt. He smacked the dog in the mouth as a bloody dew flew out and hit him in the middle of his face.

The dog lay dead in muddy waters.

Flip blew on the dog to see if it was over.

"If that don't get it, nothin' will," crowed Rooster.

"Shut up," said Flip. "Is it dead?"

"It has quit it," answered Clive.

Flip giggled: "Tee-hee. Tee-hee. Tee-hee, hee, hee." Or something like that.

Then, he broke out laughing.

"I did it, boys," he said. "I told you that I don't take no shit from anybody. I'll kick your tail in a minute if you get on my nerves."

He stepped over the dog and kicked its thang back between its legs. Then he started singing:

"You didn't know what you was messin' with. Naw, you never did. You didn't know what you was messin' with, but that's tough titty, black head."

Flip was starting to get so caught up in his own music that he mixed it.

"...because I'm bad. I'm bad. You know it. You know. And the whole wide world has to answer right now just to tell me once again—who's bad?"

Flip was a hardcore jitterbug. He had more junk in his trunk than a one-man band.

He danced in between tacklers on his way to the end zone. He had giant beads of sweat rolling off his big head and trickling down into the cracks of his skin heading toward his lips like pinballs approaching two flappers. By the time he split the trees, his laces were untied and his armpits were like mushrooms with fungi. He smelled like The Terrible Two's. He was musty, but his main concern was to start the celebration in the end zone.

"Give me a beat," he demanded.

Whenever we had to sit outside we always took a ghetto box with us, so we cranked up a special twleve-inch version of Planet Rock by Afrika Bambaataa & Soul Sonic Force and let Flip cut it up.

Flip started showing out.

"Streevus mone on the reevus cone!" he yelled.

He did the stomp, the shuffle, the bump, the black boogaloo, the Spanish hustle, the shimmy, the boogie-woogie, the Lindy hop, the bebop, the jump, the James Brown, the cootie crawl, the funky chicken, the hard bop, the Pee-Wee Herman, the running man, the M.C. Hammer, and then he did his own thang.

"Go ladies!" he sung. "I'm yo' livin' dream/love like dis/no place/turn up the base/do what ya' want/just scream-m-m!"

That's when we knew for sure he was trippin' cause there wasn't a bitch in the area.

He was point-shaving because it took him infinity to realize that the mutt had danced on his chest before kicking it.

"Look, there's scratches on my chest," Flip said. He liked to have had a baby. He acted like he was going through the changes.

"You hurt," said Clive.

"You hurtin' for certain," added Rooster.

"Spoon-feed me," said Flip.

"You need to get your act/game/program/shit together," Clive said.

"You didn't score!"

"What you talking about?" asked Flip.

"You were touched when you were down, so the play is dead right there."

"You gonna be dead if you don't shut up!" shouted Flip. "Nobody never touched me!"

Flip ran over and asked me what I thought. "Did you see somebody touch me?"

Flip was crying.

"0-bop-she-bam!" he screamed. Translated, it meant: "Lawd, save my black ass from dying and I'll promise that I'll quit shaking that thang."

"You as ugly as homemade sin," Rooster told Flip. He was adding fuel to the fire.

"That shit's gonna multiply like it does in those exorcism movies," Rooster said. "You'll be black 360 degrees then."

"Shut up, Rooster," said Clive. He was feeling sympathy for Flip's sorry-ass.

"What happened to all that talk about you being the cheese?" Clive asked.

"Yeah, you always stank," said Rooster.

"I'm gonna' kill *that muthafuckin' dog!" yelled Flip.*

Flip got mad at me because I told him that I had seen somebody touch him.

"C'mon, man, cool out," said Clive. "It's just a few scratches."

"Ask your momma for some petroleum jelly," said Rooster.

"Naw, man, he need Campo Penique," Clive said.

"Petroleum jelly," insisted Rooster.

"Campo Penique," said Clive.

"Petroleum jelly."

"Camp-po Penique!" yelled Clive.

"Where did you get a stupid idea like that from?" asked Rooster.

"My momma," said Clive.

"Your momma must have been serving fur burgers when you were hurt," said Rooster.

"The only reason why your momma uses petroleum jelly is because she's used to yo' daddy stickin' his finger up her ass," Clive said.

"You just jealous cause yo' momma got B.B.s in her cotton," said Rooster. "I heard they have to give her a relaxer before they can tag it."

"Well, at least she's got somebody else strokin' her hair instead of doing it herself like your momma do."

"No wonder your momma uses Campho Phenique," said Rooster. "She don't mind getting burned."

"You askin' for it, motherfucker!" shouted Clive.

"When I busted your momma's booty I didn't have to ask," said Rooster.

"That's because she gave you a mind-fuck," said Clive.

"I'd be the first to admit that your momma blew my mind," Rooster said, "but she blew my head first."

"You best go get that petroleum jelly then," said Clive, "cause it's starting to scab."

"At least it don't feel sore like your momma," Rooster said.

"Why don't you *shut up!" yelled Flip.*

On the next play, I decided not to throw and, instead, took off running with the ball. Flip chased me and dove savagely, driving his big head into my back. I fell to the ground and lay still. In my mind, I could see myself rolling over in pain—hitting the dirt with my fist, blades of dead grass flying up in the air and cutting across my eyes. But in reality, I knew that nothing on my body was moving.

Rooster and Clive hushed, then turned and whipped Flip with a coke stare.

"Which one do you want?" they asked. They were giving him the evil eye.

"I can take care of myself," Flip said.

"Oh yeah, what about that time you got lost in Uptown while you was carrying that fruit?" Clive asked. "I heard you crying all the way from 125th street."

"I wasn't crying," Flip said. "I was whistling."

"You was whistling 'Mommy, come get me out of here'?" asked Clive.

"I was humming 'Gone With The Wind,'" said Flip.

"Naw, man, tell it like it is," Clive said.

Flip knew that Clive-nem were starting to collar the jive, so he told us his story.

When Rooster was nine or so, we used to all sit on the stoop with boodies like charcoal and scratch house music on the cement. It was me, Clive, Rooster and three or four others—stultifying ourselves doing the independent funk-thang. Clive clung to a deck of cards, cut them, lackadaisically counted them, flipped them between his ears and pulled them out from his sleeves, performing tricks while we read books by Malcom X and Alice Walker. It was Blacks' magic. Clive would be holding Rooster's bare stomach and watching me talk almost up to the point where the spit on my lips would dry up and turn white. "Fade to black," Clive said. I didn't know why he said it. Clive's palms were the fruit of the mango; stupid-fresh juice ran off the side of his flesh, and dropped from his fingers, like it was nothing. In fact, it looked like Clive was clinging to grape jelly, with his black hand over Rooster's stomach like that, squeezin' it, dirt like bread crumbs on his face.

"This gets repetitious."

"Yes."

One day while we was doing the do outside on the stoop, it looked like somebody had killed some chickens and took an egg yolk and threw it up against a blue wall to form the sun. I was watchin' this thing drop, smearing red and yellow and mandarin orange all over the backdrop. I was caught up in melodrama and didn't even know what it was. I failed to realize that there was white people staring at me.

"Mistah Kurtz—he dead!" I heard some natives shout.

"So funky."

"Yes."

That's when I got up and decided to visit Lester W. Young.

"You all know who Lester W. Young is, don't you?"

We shook our big heads in affirmative, but not a single one of us knew who the hell he was.

"Well, anyway, in case ya' don't know, he is a very famous tenor saxophonist and he happen to be kin," Flip said.

"How he related?" we asked.

"He's my uncle."

"Everybody's your uncle, including Tom and Charlie Irvine."

Flip gave me the finger behind my back.

It felt like a spear.

"Shut up!" he said.

You see, I had promised Lester that the next time I visited him I would bring something to eat. Uncle Lester is about sixty-eight years old, so he was scoffing fishheads and searching for the gills trying to feed himself. But anyways, the only thing I could find in the house to eat was this African grape. Now I swear that I lift weights every morning but I had never carried anythang as heavy as a grape. I got about as far as Birdland and then I had to quit. So I climbed in the elevator of this nightclub in order to leave the grape where people could find it. Man. I must have went up about twenty-six floors before a couple finally got in the elevator with me. In the end, I was sorry though because this stanky bitch, who wore a straw hat, tried to crack on me.

"Look. Reggie." she said. "That boy looks like Little Black Sambo."

This man with black lizards looked at me and laughed as they went out the door talkin' about livin' easy.

"Fuck you," I said. Then I left the watermelon on the carpet and flew out the door. When I got home my momma was cooking chitlins with ham-bone soup, dumplings, crackling biscuits and sweet corn bread. Apparently we was going to eat the watermelon for dessert because she asked me right away where it was. I told her that I didn't know because I had been livin' large, but she hit me and called me a "knuckle-head" and then fired a piece of corn bread from the skillet at my big head and broke it.

"Even up until today, that's why they call it hot-water corn bread," Flip insisted with a serious look on his face.

We all stared at each other in shock.

"Where did you get a stupid lie like that from?" asked Rooster.

"You accusin' me of fibbin'?" Flip asked.

"Better yet, I'm calling you an out-and-out liar," Rooster said. "You point-shaving."

"Your momma's a liar, too," Flip replied.

"You got the nerve to talk," Rooster said. "Your momma is so ugly we got to close our eyes to listen to her."

"That's because you like wet dreams anyway."

"If your momma would wear a bra sometimes I wouldn't be having any."

"Your momma's so black she paints a white line in the middle of her booty so yo' daddy can see where to drive," Flip said.

"Yeah, well, your momma's so black she wears lights on her titties," Rooster responded.

"Your momma has to wear tennis shoes so you can find her in the dark," said Flip.

"You so black you drink white milk so you can see yo' pee," Rooster cackled.

"It's going to be me and you if you keep talking," Flip said.

"If you feel froggy, leap!" shouted Rooster.

"That did it!" shouted Flip. He was ready to get down dirty/ fonky/foul and shitty. "I know you ain't trying to talk because your big, fat Bahamma momma ain't doin' nuttin' but sitting on her black behind waiting for your daddy to take care of you and that's why you ain't got no clothes or nuttin' cause your daddy's out screwing white horses and your momma's too stupid to realize it and that's the reason why he be beating on her because she be cooking and ironing and cleaning and doing all of that stuff for him and don't care what he doing, cause if she did you wouldn't be living in that one-room shack with the one window that's busted and the wood boards that be falling all in your yard which you ain't got the decency to put any grass in and that's why you be illin' all the time cause you just mad that your daddy lives in a jungle like a gorilla whenever your parents get together."

When Flip had finished, my momma walked out of the house and stood on the porch with a spatula in her hand. I heard her coming; she moves like a cold front.

"Listen here, you little nappy-head boy!" she said. "You got no business talking out here like that after what you did to Jimmie. I'm getting sick and tired of hearing your mouth and your lies. If your momma or daddy cared anything about you, you wouldn't be out here acting the way you do. If it wasn't for your momma, you wouldn't be here in the first place. But, because she went ahead and got knocked up, we got to look at your ugly face. If it wasn't for the fact that Jimmie enjoys seeing Clive and Rooster around, I'd sweep your dusty little behind off the porch and tell you to go home, so you ought to be glad that I can't control who they choose for their friends. Now sit your little ass down and shut up before I slap you in the mouth."

Momma was steamin' as the storm shot over our heads.

"Shoot," Momma said to Flip. "Look what you done did to him."

"Why won't you talk?" Rooster whispered to me.

"Play misty for me," I wanted to say to Rooster.

Rooster wrapped his arms around my body and pushed me further underneath the roof as I watched Flip lower his big head and stroll away, clutching his bottle of Mad Dog in the dizzy rain.

Rooster tossed up a handful of sand and it came back down as mud. "I like your momma," he said.

Shit On Alondra

ALONDRA BLED REAL
black blood mixed with 10W-40 oil and hard water as I walked
down the street during the Rodney King beating. The LAPD kicked
King's ass, causing him to let go of a bomb that hit me in the face.
The coppers spat on him, insulted him, whupped his big head
with their gas masks at hand and stuck black-eyed peas on King's
face.

King reached out and touched me: This is what I would say on
the David Letterman show about my brush with greatness.
Letterman would probably add a writer's embellishment: "The
moment King touched me, I knew that his big head was in trouble.
He looked up and shouted that he needed ham hocks for the
policeman's benefit dinner." I would tell no one the truth, that
King farted in my face.

Brothers and sisters cursed the cops and called them whips and
pinks as King held on to my stress fracture.

"Save me!" cried King. There were beans rolling down Alondra's
hips and pork rinds falling out of King's pockets, the Pigs treating
him like slop.

"Get away from me!" I shouted. "There's nothing I can do!"

Residents of Compton fired fresh eggs at the police and
watched them bust open on the street like white people's heads

cracked against the hot pavement, their brains on the ground battered and yellow and covered by black pepper as they fried. The boys pushed Rodney King in the back, and he rolled over and kissed Alondra with his big lips. The cops shoved me away. "Move the crowd," said Charlie Irvine, "before this gets ugly." Six or seven cops beat him like it was nothing. King let go of a dozen more gastric bombs while the rioting intensified.

"The police stank!" residents shouted. I pointed to King with his booty up in the air and lips bleeding. He turned over on his side and looked up at me.

"This is war," he said. "Save me from my enemies."

"War," said a prostitute. "What is it good for?"

"Love is its antecedent," I answered.

"Oh," she said. "I understand, now that you put it that way."

Meantime, two policemen got hit by bombs and fell out. People cracked up. The LAPD radioed for help, but police chief Daryl Gates informed them that twenty of his best officers were manhandling Zsa-Zsa Gabor.

"Backup is unavailable," said Gates. "You'll have to take care of the devil yourself."

"Why so many men and bones for Zsa-Zsa?" Charlie Irvine's uncle, Tom, asked.

"What are you, stupid or something?" Gates asked. "Over."

"What are you doing to her?" asked Tom.

"Why you care why? Over."

"What are you doing?" asked Tom. "I need to know."

"We're pumping her," said Gates. "Over."

"I thought you wanted Diana Ross," said Tom.

"She was too skinny to fuck. Over."

"What do we do with King?" asked Tom.

"Give him the sweet dream he's been asking for and beat him. Over."

"Will you back us up?" asked Tom.

"I've already fucked you. Over."

"Don't be funny," said Tom.

"Put Charlie back on the mike and chill. Over."

"Why can't I join in on the fun?" asked Tom.

"Your penis is like a teacher's piece of white chalk. It's too little to do it. Over."

"It's not! Over!"

"Give me that!" Charlie Irvine said. He snatched the receiver out of Tom's hands. "You're getting carried away!"

Tom looked as if his feelings had been hurt. Charlie Irvine leaned over and gave him a warm-fuzzy.

"You alright?" Charlie Irvine asked.

Tom swallowed some alcohol from a bottle inside the glove department of a black-and-white.

"Don't worry about me. You can't hurt your Uncle Tom."

Tom held on to the bottle with his big, black hands and spat a hot fever on King's forehead.

Charlie Irvine kissed the ground that Tom walked on, his thin white lips marred by gravel.

"You're the man," said Charlie Irvine. "Do the do."

Tom ran over and busted the bottle on King's big head, alcohol running down Alondra's ass like a fresh screwdriver.

"Oh yeah," said another cop as King rolled around Alondra's curves like a smashed Corvette.

Alondra was bloody and dirty, an arm of the road bruised by tracks and marks as if a black female junkie had staged her own accident.

"Let me die with my woman!" King shouted. He was ossified and out of it and talking out the side of his neck.

King's black girlfriend ran up to him and spat in his face.

"I should have left yo' ass a long time ago!" she yelled. Then she sprinted away from the scene of the crime.

"Bitch!" King shouted. "You mine when I catch you!"

"Shut this nigger up!" Tom shouted.

A copper stepped up and threw gasoline all over Rodney King's body. As King rolled around screaming, the cop whipped out a matchbook, and each of the officers snatched a match and lit it.

Then they burnt King the fuck up.

King looked up at me like it was my fault.

"You ain't shit," he said.

"This whole shit to finish you off was out of my hands," I replied. "It was a bowel movement which was caused by sickness and virtually unstoppable."

King put his chest up against Alondra, the dark tarred pebbles feeling like hard nipples underneath his skin.

"Black is beautiful!" shouted King in a last hurrah while burning up.

A Compton woman cracked an egg on his back before the flames died.

Horrors hung out by the wire trash cans which were like fish nets on the edges of the street. Black pimps and hookers and charlatans became tuna, cat, mackerel, largemouth and walleye staring at me as I sailed past the seamier areas of Compton, Alondra leading me on as my guide.

The matchbook skipped in the breeze like it was caught in a game of hopscotch or caught in Scotch period. A naked white woman tried to play dead on the lacquered cover, but a high gloss in her eyes suggested that she was stoned, like a bloody Mary. She had been burned between her legs, her nipples shot by firepower, each pointing out of the barrel of her breast like the tip of a large bullet. I hopped, skipped and jumped to snatch her off the street before she went off. She was headed for the gutter, bouncing along the sleepless night as if she were just a shell of the woman she wanted to be. I plugged the hole between her legs with my finger and watched her as if plumbing were my occupation. She bent over like a dancing girl, showing her pale booty which was like a leaky toilet trickling water down her leg. Rain spattered like a light drink doused in my face, the wet dancing girl doing everything she could to snap me out of it.

"I wouldn't waste my time fucking around with that if I were you," Jimmy said. Jimmy hung out in the slums like a jitterbug. He

introduced himself as Jimmy Cricket, grass in his mouth.
"It ain't no good," he said. "I threw it away." Jimmy talked while
rolling a J in Tops. He put the joint into a Kool cigarette box. The
Kool box was filled with big suckers wrapped in psychedelic
papers. Jimmy was an artificial nigger.

"What are you going to do with all that dope?" I asked.

Jimmy slid his fingers through his gray, matted hair and divided
it. "I'll do whatever you want me to do," he said. He was a man
with a vice, and it had screwed his head into a pleasure dome.

"You ain't going to do nothing," I said to Jimmy. "You're a liar,
a dirty punk."

"Give me back my matchbook!" Jimmy yelled.

I pulled the matchbook away from him. "Go home!" I shouted.

Jimmy staged his own murder. He lowered his big head right
there, clean out in the middle of the street, and frowned. His head
looked like a dented globe, his face dripping water and covered
with tattoos.

I ran like never before.

The cold night dragged along slowly as a snake when it sheds its
skin. I drifted aimlessly, my huge black hands clutching the brown
bottle, flickering flames from lit matches following me wherever.
I sauntered past the flats of Compton and stopped in the slow rain
to hear Willie blow the basic blues with his golden-brass horn as
he sat erect on Alondra's flat ass. Willie was determined to not let
the street get away from him, the dark hard life of Compton inside
sunny California turning people into lemons piled on a step.

With no shirt on, I leaned against a wooden bench and watched
a fruit truck pull up and carry people away. For pennies, these
people jumped aboard. "It's pure hell," each one of the passengers
seemed to be saying as they rode away with their black gloves high
in the air and squeezed into fists.

"Aren't you a fruit picker?" somebody asked.

"Yes, unfortunately," I replied. "I've picked fruits all of my life."

Somebody looked at me like why-aren't-you-on-the-truck-then.

While watching Willie, a drop of rain ran down the bridge of my nose like a drunk driver, went off the edge and hit Alondra. Before putting on my jacket, I lifted the bottle to my lips and tasted the warm and bitter alcohol, which rested on the smooth, fat glass.

Willie was blowing a mean tune: I imagined a spectrum of colors slowly rising out of his horn in linear fashion and then bending over into a rainbow. In the rain, his music was like easy listening, hip-hop rap. His music seduced me, made love to my mind. It seemed like Willie was playing in a fantastical atmosphere of fuchsia. Colors of deep purple and red surfaced into bruises and kisses on his cheek. This gave Willie an odd blush as he blew into the metal while caressing the yellow brass in his soft hands as if the horn were his woman.

Two prostitutes gossiped in front of me.

Suddenly both women broke off their conversation, whirled around and looked at me. The soft rain changed into mist as we stared at each other silently.

"Your fly is open," said one of the women. Her moist nipples looked like old pennies as they grew in size under her thin white blouse.

"You wanna fuck?" she asked. She was an around-the-way girl.

"No, I want you to piss on yourself," I said. Well, I didn't exactly say it, but that's what I was thinking.

"Do the toilet thang," I whispered. She didn't hear me.

My penis wiggled a bit inside my pants. "You just mad cause you pissed on yourself," it said. I was sorry I made it talk.

"Shut up!" I said. I could feel it droop as if its feelings were hurt.

The other woman looked at me with a question mark in her eye. "Aren't you DJ Quik?" she asked.

"Can he spin?" I asked.

"What difference does it make?" she said.

"Has he sexed you up?" I asked.

"Hasn't everyone?" she asked. "South Central LA is chock full of gangs, bad fuckers and fruit pickers."

The question mark in her eye was a fishhook specifically

intended for catching black cat.

"Are you a bad fucker?" she asked.

"I'm a fruit picker," I said.

"Are you a cherry picker?" she asked.

"No, just a fruit picker," I replied.

"You've been around then," she said.

"I was born and raised in Compton," I replied.

"You wanna fuck?" she asked. She dug in my pants for money.

"Get away from me!" I shouted. "You don't know what you're doing!"

I stuck the bottle inside the pocket of my black jacket and stared at the curves on Alondra. Alondra—with dirt sidewalks and slender legs, leaky sewers and taped up arms, old newspaper and bad joints, stinky dark alleys and big ass, oily bumps and black skin, perverted sex licking and big lips—had changed. Alondra was dope. To residents of Compton, Alondra was lady heroine. When I was young, there were lemon and orange trees on Alondra which mingled with the flats and sometimes embraced them. There were block parties, sweet barbecue cooked over hot charcoal. Now Alondra had become hardcore. Twelve at night, a group of black kids with "Dreamboys" on their jackets played stickball like their lives were on the line; they focused on swinging the piece of wood just right so that they could smack the face of the white ball hard enough to send it flying through a window.

"Do you wanna fuck or not?" the woman asked. "There is no time for nostalgia. I got a business going on here."

I was zoning. I assumed that the two women had moved the crowd, but she jolted me back into reality. I had been running down the hood of Alondra for a reason, but couldn't remember what it was.

I rolled, then wobbled away. I hit the porch of a brick building like a Cadillac hubcap. The building was one of a slew of flats lined up; it read "1307" on a side marred by graffiti. The walls and me mixed like Cream of Wheat and brown sugar.

"Do you know what you are?" the woman asked. "You're sick!"

Her voice bounced off the building like a beach ball.

I knocked on the door.

"Wait! Stop!" shouted someone. He was graying and dressed like a modern-day court jester.

"What?"

"You'd rather fuck my mind instead of me, wouldn't you?" she shouted.

"Will you give me a penny for my thoughts?" he asked. He held out his hands. His chewed fingernails were painted in different colors, and his palms were dyed green and yellow.

"Get away from me, fool," I said. He smiled as if that were flattery.

He had on large, oversized boat shoes and rouge all over his face. There were holes all in his clothes, and his kneecap stuck out through the blue material like a small mountain. He wore a Dodgers' baseball cap on his big head.

"I see you like my hat," he said. "I got it out of the can over there. Oh, the slings of fortune...."

"There's nothing better in life than being a Dodger."

"Why did you come over here and mess with me?" I asked.

"It takes a fool to know one. Ha!" he said. Then he reached into the front pockets of his plaid pants while moving his hands around and pretended to search for something.

"Say, you wouldn't happen to have a quarter, would you? It seems as if I have lost mine."

"Who are you to call me names?" I asked. I tried to ignore the fact that he was a beggar.

"Who are you to ask?" he responded.

"Poof!" he said for no reason at all.

The rain stopped momentarily.

"You play too much," I told him. "You've been watching too many Laker games and point guards. There's only one Magic show."

He grabbed my hand, squeezing my fingers softly, and pointed it toward the moon.

"The world is a stage, and the stage is a circus, so somebody has to be the clown," he said. His voice boomed in dramatic fashion as he stared at both me and the sky.

I jerked my hand away. "Very good," I said. The sky and the clouds were like ambrosia salad to me, a home-sweet-home for fruits and marshmallows.

"You're too soft for me," I said. I was trying to give him a hint.

"Thank you, my lord. Ha!" he said. Then he bowed in front of me, but was careful not to close his eyes. However, I followed his repulsive glances and saw that my zipper had broken open again. I quickly zipped it back up while he stood watching me. His eyes appeared to be obsidian pieces in the moonlight. They shimmied as if the earth beneath them was unstable.

"Art thou too cruel to thyself?" he asked. "It'll suffocate in there like that."

I tossed him a quarter and watched the silver glisten as it spun a tornado. "Take it and leave me alone before I kick your fun-filled ass," I said. And for the first time, he was offended.

"There can be no kernel inside this light nut," he said. Then he turned and strolled away, leaving the quarter on a clump of dead grass.

I went over to pick it up but noticed something else in the weeds and stickers and stuff. I grabbed it and set it on my palm for observation. Whatever it was, it made for elementary study— a flat round base the size of a half-dollar and a clear glass cylinder with yellow liquid. The cylinder attached itself to one side of the base; there was a small air bubble inside.

I tilted and shook it in an attempt to position the bubble in the middle of the cylinder as it rested on the palm of my left hand.

"Use your right brain to center the bubble," I said to myself. I was slightly out of it.

"Shut up, homeboy," I heard the left part of my brain say.

"I know you're not talking to me," said the right brain.

"Who else would I be talking to?" asked the left brain.

"Your mama," said the right brain.

"That did it!" said the left brain. Both sides started fighting, spitting blood and pounding each other against the cranium like it was nothing.

I grabbed my forehead and squeezed it like an orange. "Quit," I said.

"Throw his ass out in the street!" screamed the right brain.

"It takes two to make a thang go right!" I shouted.

With a headache, I tried to relocate the bubble. But just at the moment when the bubble had almost reached the middle, another thought dawned on me.

"Why am I always trying to balance things in my life?" I asked. The bubble slid back and forth inside the glass, forcing me to remember why I had been stomping down Alondra.

"Sometimes it seems as if I never have control of my life," said Jasmine. She had a drink in her hands, and a napkin stuck to the bottom of the glass as she spoke.

She had fruit in her drink, which made me ponder about why she was confused. "Sometimes," "maybe," "seems." They all suggested a kind of indifference, an admittance that she had already thrown in the towel.

"I just don't give a fuck," she suggested. "You can take that anyway you want."

The rhythm and blues music slowed down into a tempo more suitable for a waltz. I decided to ask her for a dance then.

She cheesed. "You've got your mind on booty," she said.

I looked innocent. "Boogie," I said. "All I want to do is boogie."

"This is nothing but foreplay," she said, "since we both know that if a man has any skills at all he can play with a woman's booty while on the dance floor."

"Well, you're the one who said that I could take my fuck anyway I want."

"You ask for it," she said.

She set the wet glass on the table, stood up, smiled and then headed for the dance floor. I walked slow; she walked fast. I was unable to catch her until we reached an open area in front of a wall of mirrors.

"Let's see what you got," she said, tripping.

"I'm the boogie-man," I responded. "When I do my thang, people watch me and shudder."

"You're a shit-talker," she said. "A jerker."

We touched each other awkwardly to position ourselves. People dancing around us parked themselves like fire trucks in case of an emergency.

"Feel the passion," I said to Jasmine. The statement sounded like promotional advertisement for The Movie Channel.

"Make me sweat," Jasmine replied.

I tried to pull her closer, breathe on her, smell the side of her neck. We banged knees, stepped on one another's ankles and tried to kill each other. We cut the rug. Then the music stopped.

"Give it up!" I said.

She waltzed away. She smiled and retraced her steps, bouncing up-and-down like a balloon which had been turned loose. I tried to follow her, but she walked very fast/I walked slow. I lost control of her. She sprinted to the table, sat down facing me, crossed her legs and sipped from her drink. She wore a skirt down to her thighs, her legs covered with fish net.

A tall, muscular man wearing Brutini loafers moved over from a nearby chair and hit on her. His face was like a moldy piece of white bread.

She ate it up. He got down on his hands and knees and begged for some action.

"Whatever you want," she said.

He pulled the chair out from under her, and she darted past a huge area of activity. The black women were schooled and busting any fishermen who tried to play like they were single.

"Don't even try it, honey," said Cleopatra Jones. Everything was on the surface. She called Jasmine a little tramp behind her back.

"Girl," Cleopatra said to her best friend. "I would take her man in a minute if he had the sense to catch me when she's not around."

Neither Jasmine nor the white man heard her. They danced like a couple of figure skaters spinning on their toes. I wasn't sure which one I wanted to fall first, but if I had had a slingshot I would have tried to take both of them out together. I took them to be a joke: She pranced around like she was baking cookies, and he flexed his muscle, hitting on her time and time again.

"What you need is a drink," I said to myself. I ordered several of them. First, I ordered amaretto stone sours. But they tasted like lemonade. Lemonade reminded me of citrus fruits. Citrus fruits reminded me of sunlight. Sunlight reminded me of flowers. And, flowers forced me to think about Jasmine.

"Fuck these," I said to myself. Then I stopped a waitress who was floating about carrying a round platter of short and tall, dark brown bottles.

"Amaretto stone sours are too light," I said. "People will only think that I'm drunk. Bring me some beer."

"What's wrong?" the waitress asked. "You look pale."

"Paleness is a white thang," I said.

I finally reached the point where I could no longer stand to watch Jasmine. The bottle encouraged me to leave.

"Don't worry about a thang," I heard it say, its smooth mouth and big lips salivating. "You'll never be alone as long as I'm here. Just make sure that you keep me with you. You'll do that, won't you?"

I shook my big head and grabbed the bottle and then flew out the door, noticing that the sweet and spicy scent of Jasmine was still on my black jacket.

"Two is a crowd!" said the right brain. "Get rid of the other side before it's too late!"

"Don't listen to that right winger!" the left brain yelled. "He doesn't even have a girlfriend!"

"Both of you shut up!" I shouted, stumbling off the side of the porch.

Clive opened the door and stared at me like I was crazy.

"What's happening?" he asked.

"I'm buggin' out," I answered.

"Join the party," Clive said.

I went inside and saw Rooster, Bosco and Carlos hanging around in the living room. Carlos' neck was red, like it had been colored with lipstick.

Clive dove down on the carpet, acting as though he thought the grease on his bald head was balm, like it belonged on the ball of an antiperspirant.

"Go ahead…rub it," he urged. We all put our hands on his big head and made like he was our Swami. We felt the braille on his scalp.

"Cool the fever and ease the pain!" Rooster shouted. Rooster's daddy used to be a Baptist preacher.

We all shined Clive's head some more and made primitive noises. Clive was moody. He shrugged us off after starting the stuff.

"Look, no ash!" cried Bosco, holding his hands out so everyone could see.

"I'm bleeding," Carlos whined.

"You a fool for cutting your head," Clive's momma said. Rooster trotted over to be close to her.

"What you fixing?" Rooster asked. He leaned over to delve into the black skillet on the stove, hoping to steal some meat.

"Sweet potatoes," Bosco said. "I smell 'em."

"Your momma looks like she can throw down," Rooster said to Clive.

Clive pretended to ignore him. He slapped yellow hair wax on his head and rolled over on the floor to grab a wooden hair brush underneath the sofa.

"It takes a lot of nerve to use a brush on that head," said Bosco. "It's as tender as lettuce."

Clive rolled all around the couch and did a 360.

"Gracious, why are you rolling around like that?" Carlos asked.

"I saw a mouse on the floor," Clive replied. He owned a young

Afghan hound with brown hair, and it trotted past the arm of the sofa as he spoke.

"Goodness!" Carlos screamed. "Stop that dog from eating the thing!"

"I can't stop him," said Clive, joking. "He's too hungry."

"Heavens! I can't understand what kind of dog would swallow rodents!"

"What's wrong with dead mice?" Bosco asked.

"I wouldn't touch those things!" shouted Carlos.

"They ain't nothing but fur," Bosco said.

"I'm scared of you," Carlos added.

"So, who'd expect courage from you anyway?" Bosco asked.

Carlos twisted his body to accentuate his nether parts and then stuck out his middle finger and flagged it.

"You ain't got nothing no ways, you old, skinny-looking feline," said Bosco, wiping his hair with a paper towel because he was hot.

"You wish you had some, black boy," Carlos said.

Bosco blew up.

"If you had any meat, it would smell like chitlins," Bosco said.

"I'd rather be a pig than a black boy," Carlos said. Then he called Bosco uncouth and walked away. It sounded kind of seddity. Snooty, that is.

"What he say?" Bosco asked.

"Don't ask me," said Clive, his tongue out a la Michael Jordan.

"Tongue me," joked Carlos from a good distance.

"Faggot," said Bosco.

"As you like it, honey," Carlos said.

"You going to screw her?" asked Rooster, referring to Carlos. Rooster likes to have cheap thrills.

"She might be burning," said Bosco. He didn't have enough sense to know when to shut up.

Rooster cracked up. He looked like a devil who had just snatched a soul. Carlos went twitching into the deepest, darkest corner of the kitchen in order to be left alone. I rested my back against the wall and started picking off pieces of dried enamel. A few paint chips landed on the floor, crushed themselves and split into hundreds of smaller pieces. Ten roaches broke at top speed across the room, and one had the nerve to stop at my big toe and look up at me. It raised its egg sack straight up in the air. Then it flew.

"You a punk," I whispered.

Clive fingered his head like he was walking through the yellow pages, trying to figure me out.

"Hey Clive, don't it take more than eighty days to go round your head?" crowed Rooster. "At the rate you going, we'll die before we see you complete the trip."

"Shut up," Clive snapped, and Rooster and Bosco started making primitive noises again, the room full of woo-woo's .

"You got a head like the moon," Bosco contorted, "ain't nothing but craters."

"You want to eat, don't you?" asked Clive.

"I'm just joking," said Bosco.

"Then keep your big ass shut," Clive penciled on a small pad of white paper covered by graffiti. He showed it to Bosco.

"I was just kidding," said Bosco. "You ain't gotta have a baby about it."

"You mine when I find your ass," I whispered.

Clive looked at me and scratched his head. "Let's go for a walk," he said.

I got up, and we left.

Alondra was quiet while me and Clive walked along the curb talking stuff.

"I got a woman pregnant," Clive said. We crossed the intersection.

"Getting a woman pregnant is a delicate situation," I said. We turned around in order to work our way back, both of us upset and nervous, walking on egg shells.

"I don't know how I did it," Clive said.

"Did you fuck her?" I asked.

Clive nodded his big head.

"How many times?"

Clive started counting with his fingers, and then he quit and shook his head.

"I don't know," he said.

"Damn man, wasn't once enough?" I asked. We passed by a stop sign, leaning on one another.

"It seemed so easy," Clive said.

"What did?" I asked.

"What should I do?" Clive asked.

"Did she suck you in?"

"I did it!" Clive shouted. "I did it!"

"You gotta be concerned with more than just doing it," I responded.

We strolled past an orange sign that read "ROAD UNDER CONSTRUCTION," each of us with an arm on the other's shoulder.

"What should I do?" Clive asked.

"Are you sure she's pregnant?"

"Why would she lie?"

"Don't ask me," I replied.

"What should I do?" Clive asked.

"What makes you think it was you who made her pregnant?" We approached a traffic light, hesitated but kept going, our big heads bouncing up and down.

"She's not the type who would fool around."

"There's a kid in everyone," I said.

"I should have never fucked her," Clive said. We kicked an egg out of our way and headed towards home.

"What should I do?" Clive asked.

"Do the right thang," I answered. "Do the right thang."

"What you mean?" Clive asked.

"Why don't you just fess up?" I said.

"What should I do?" Clive asked. "What should I do?"

"Look out for the rotten egg."

Clive veered to the left, and we tiptoed around the King-size heap-pile, side-stepping a slew of eggs and shattering pieces of glass.

A Black woman driving a Dodge Dart ran over the pile and crashed. She was a nervous wreck, King underneath her tires begging for more.

"Come on, baby," King said. "Give it to me."

"I am," she said. "So then I can leave yo' ass for good."

Clive looked down at his pants. "This whole thang is a trip," he said.

Make A Thang Go Right

"I USTA SIT AND WONDER where I'd be," Rachel said, "but then the day came and gone and I finally started saying fuck them if they don't give a damn about me and my kind."

LeRoy rubbed his big head and ran his finger through his frizzled hair, looking perplexed while she had a baby.

"Who you talking about?" he asked. He was confused, and she seemed to talking out the side of her neck.

"It don't matter anymore who they is," she said. "All I know is that they don't want my babies to live because they're Niggers and my babies would just as soon get stepped on and die before they get any help in this place."

Rachel reared her head back and spat out another baby.

"That one's blacker than the other one," LeRoy said, wondering what fucking place she was talking about.

"Ain't one of 'em no different," she insisted. "You seen one, you done seen them all. I don't even care what they look like anymore. It don't make a difference. They all look alike anyway." Rachel was spewing out black minstrel shit.

"What you gonna' call that one?" LeRoy asked. He touched the baby and his fingers got wet.

"I ain't even got time to worry about it," she said. "Fuck it. What

difference does it make? They ain't nothin' but Niggers anyway."
She spat out another one.

"Why don't you stop. You look tired."

"Boy, are you muthafuckin' crazy? What makes you think I can afford to stop? Public aid don't care how many I have. So why should you?"

He winced.

"Wipe your mouth," he said. "There's tar all over your lips."

"Shit, I ain't doin' nothin'," she said. "I'm going to stay just the way I is. You can kiss me where the sun don't shine—and where it rains everyday—as far I'm concerned. If you don't like it, put rocks on my lips. Maybe that will shut my mouth, but nobody asked you to bring your black ass in here and start asking questions."

She felt a lump in her throat.

"I'll stop talking when I'm good and ready," she said.

"You through?" he asked. He felt like her taxi driver.

"Not yet," she replied. She was enjoying the ride.

LeRoy wanted to kill the conversation. He was silent while Rachel battered him with a lot of smack.

"I don't know where you get off trying to tell me what to do anyway," she said. "You ain't the one fucking with me. You need to keep your big ass out of it. You ain't gone do nothin' but get yo'self hurt, boy."

LeRoy leaned up against the wall, twirling a corncob in his left hand and jingling loose change in the other. Rachel sat in a large velvet-cushioned reclining chair and spread her legs to show him a Venus flytrap in action.

"Quit screwing around," said LeRoy.

She spat out another baby which smacked the wall and fell to the floor.

"You kilt it," said LeRoy.

"So I did. What you, a copper or something?" she asked.

LeRoy fondled the corn, enjoying the feel of Parkay on his fingers. "I don't know what I am," he said. Then he crept over to the window and looked outside. He saw Clive, Rooster and Clayborn hunched around a broken street sign. Clive was rubbing his big head and eight-sixing salesmen left and right, while Rooster and Clayborn leaned on the street pole as if it were a spear between them.

"What you lookin' at?" Rachel asked.

"Nothin."

"It's raining like hell, isn't it?"

"Yeah."

"Good—business is closed today then."

LeRoy stared at the big, brown lips of her vagina like he had never seen sex before.

Another sucker popped out of her mouth and hit him in the face. He wiped his eyes and nose and stepped on it, squishing blood up against his pants leg.

"Shut up, gawddammit!" said LeRoy, who dropped his cob and crept towards the door.

"Where you goin'?"

"To hell," he said. He saw the red light in front of her window.

"The road to hell is paved with priests' skulls," she said. There was nothing but gum and red between her teeth as she laughed at him.

"I gotta go," he said. Then he flew out the door, looking like he had rouge on his face.

"What happened?" Clive asked. "Did you get it?"

"Yeah, I got it," LeRoy answered.

"What did it look like?" asked Rooster.

"Like bush," LeRoy said. "There was black hair everywhere, all in between her legs."

"Was it rough?" asked Rooster.

"It was coarse."

"But how did it feel when you poked it?" asked Rooster.

"It felt like sandpaper and needles glued together by Elmer's," said LeRoy.

"How much was it?" asked Clive.

"Twenty dollars."

"Was it worth it?"

"Uh-huh."

"Did she have big titties?" Rooster asked.

"Uh-huh."

"Were her nipples black?"

"Did she scream when you poked it?"

"No."

"That figures, doesn't it, Clive? She's been banged so much that it doesn't make sense for her to scream."

"What makes you believe that?" LeRoy asked.

"Clayborn's got a calculator," Rooster replied.

"What's he doing with it?"

"Statistics," Rooster replied.

"So," said LeRoy.

"So that's how I know," said Rooster.

"Settle down, Rooster," said Clive. "You're sick in the head. A normal man wouldn't be shaking his ding-a-ling like that."

"You actin' like a gorilla," LeRoy said.

"That's because that momma has got a jungle," Rooster said. "I bet she's got chickens and shit running around."

"Don't point," Clive said. "She might see you."

"I want to go home," LeRoy said.

"Not so fast," said Rooster.

"What's the matter?" asked Clayborn.

"You look like you've seen the devil," said Clive.

"You wanna go down the street for more wings and thangs and corn-on-the-cob?" asked Rooster.

"Later," said LeRoy. "I wore it out."

"What did you do to it?" asked Rooster.

"I bumped her booty hard until I reached the point where I almost dropped dead."

"How did you break the ice with her?" asked Clive.

"I asked her why she was a whore."

"What did she say?" asked Clive.

"Nothing," said LeRoy. He played with a couple of nickel-dimes inside his pants pockets.

"Was she sore when you left?" asked Rooster.

"Why don't you quit asking me questions," said LeRoy. "Raindrops keep falling on my big head."

"Let's go," said Clayborn. "It's starting to get blacker out here."

"Let's go before things get worser," said Rooster.

Rooster, Clive and Clayborn moved the crowd. LeRoy took the blue line home, holding on to his trembling umbrella and eating apples. Metro Rail was the future, but the blue line was in effect, busing Negroes dirt-cheap. The ride sounded like vampire bats inside a cave. His teeth shimmied, chewing on pieces of skin. Cool breeze shot pool, borrowing cues from the passengers' heads. People leaned and bumped each other.

"Rocky-road ice cream is what I want!" a white woman behind LeRoy loudly proclaimed. She wore a smock. No, a dashiki. No, a handkerchief. No, a white napkin with "dare to travel" written on it. No, a silk pullover by Guess with a V-cut in the back. Whatever it was, it was scented with White Shoulders-Tabu-Cinnabar-Opium-Eternity-Obsession. And several buttons on it were broke.

"Let it all hang out," some man whispered.

The metal hooks in the ceiling clanged as they knocked each other around with the movement of transportation.

"Feel here," she said. She moved his big, black hand inside her legs, and he let it go while discussing "Sweet Dick Willie" in her ears. He talked drag.

The bus traveled stop-and-go, walking a thin line between love and hate.

People rushed in and out of the glass doors, handing the driver yen and shit. The man and woman let go of the rail and strolled to the exit.

"Time to go," said the man.

"The party's over," declared the woman.

The passengers escaped through the crowd with their hands in their pockets and faces to the curb, mud and brown water babies running into the gutter like junkies trying to hide.

LeRoy discovered the sports section of the newspaper and checked to see how the Dodgers were hitting. LeRoy saw a man put a bomb in his mouth and light it. He cracked up. It was a Bob Marley, bigger-than-life joint.

LeRoy grinned. A man peered over his shoulder and whispered in his ears.

"Wanna get blowed?"

"Say no to drugs," LeRoy said. He had read the slogan on the brim of a Lemonhead. The wheels of the bus got screechy, like they were rolling over laughing.

The man looked at LeRoy like he was crazy.

"What are you talking about?" he asked. "I'm talkin' about getting yo' fucking dick wet."

"Get out of here!" LeRoy shouted.

"I'll do you for free," the man said.

"Get you a fuckin' lollipop," LeRoy said.

"Got one!" the man said. He snatched a cherry blowpop out of his pocket and gave it to LeRoy.

"What's your problem?" LeRoy asked.

"You circumcised?" the man asked.

"You a freak or something?"

"I don't want my teeth to slip off your dick. You wouldn't feel it that way."

"Don't make me bust you in the mouth."

"What?"

"You heard me! Bug off, you queer!"

"Black nigger!"

"You're sick," said LeRoy.

"Homosexuality is not a disease," the man said.

"It's not the same as being black either," LeRoy said.

"Which one is worse?" asked the man.

"What you mean?" asked LeRoy.

"Which one would you rather be?" asked the man.

"Black," said LeRoy. "Black as the roof inside your mouth when it's closed."

"Why?" asked the man. "Tell me why."

"One mean something wrong on the outside, but the other mean something wrong on the inside," LeRoy said.

"Which is which?" asked the man.

"You ought to know," replied LeRoy. "You the one who called me a black nigger."

"You need to make wholesale changes with your episteme," said the man. "I'm gone. You're nothin' but a prick."

"Episteme," LeRoy said. "What's that?"

The man faded into the back of the bus. His knees buckled as the bus spurted forward, its headlights looking like fangs as it glided down the dark roadway making noise.

LeRoy laid the paper across his lap and stared out the window. He felt himself getting sleepy as the bus moved along, his neck stiff and sore and as dead as a tube of lipstick.

He leaned back and let the blood rush to his neck. Then he dropped his big head and went to sleep.

"I'll bet the nipples on her boobs are gigantic," said Rooster. He happily skipped over squares while Clive-nem left tracks on the wet cement of the sidewalk.

"Shut up!" said Clive. Then he gave Rooster the evil eye.

"I've seen the face of evil, and it looks like Clive Barker!" exclaimed Rooster. He wanted to see *Hellraiser*.

"Count me out," said Clayborn. Then he left.

"What do ya wanna do now?" Rooster asked.

"Nothing," said Clive. "Let's go home."

Clive looked like a totem pole in the black rain. His eyes were shining as he muttered mumbo-jumbo to himself and ate JuJu's in the face of the wind.

"Your teeth are gonna rot eatin' on all that candy," said Rooster.

"You just jealous," Clive replied.

The two walked away from the liquor store with Rooster talking some stew about trying to get even or something like that and tearing open a plastic container full of Tic-Tacs.

Clayborn would be hyped if he learned to express himself more, LeRoy thought. His big head was propped up against the dull wall of the bus like a dill pickle in a glass jar.

LeRoy sat still as a basin—oceans in his body, his neck wiggling like jellied cranberry sauce dumped from a dented can.

LeRoy felt faint. As the bus shook his neck, he almost passed out.

LeRoy stopped what he was doing and leaned over to the other side of the bus, swells in his neck.

"I bet if I fucked her I could make her scream," Rooster said. He wiped the rain off his face and combed his hair as they waltzed past the hospital, roses all over the place.

"Get off it!" Clive shouted. "I am sick and tired of talking about her."

"What's wrong?" Rooster asked.

"All you ever talk about is sex," Clive said.

"What else is there to talk about?" Rooster asked.

Rooster squeezed on the condom inside his pocket and felt the lubrication shoot through a pinhole in the wrapping like blood. He hopped and skipped along the sidewalk, crushing flowers in his way.

"One, two, three, crack!" Rooster said to himself. "One, two, three, crack!"

Clive looked at him what-in-the-world-was-he-doing.

"Have you ever tried a hospital in Compton?" Clive asked.

Rachel sat in the chair talking rhetoric to herself. She dropped Visine in her eyes and rubbed them. They ended up looking like cin- namon disks that had been put in someone's mouth and sucked on.

It was black like the inside of a covered trash can while Clive and Rooster walked around in the ghetto–starving.

Clive stood in muddy waters, Rooster stomping puddles by the hospital entrance to the emergency room, splashing rhythms together like John Coltrane.

Clive pointed above his big head.

"The moon is a lozenge rolling back and forth and the stars are chocolate in the darkness," he said.

Rooster had to add his two cents.

"The big, black hole in the sky is for sex," Rooster said, "and the trees are for nuts and honey."

An ambulance raced past them and to the emergency room. The noise was a fat lady singing.

Rooster and Clive heard screams. Screams, screams, screams. Long screams. Clayborn running away from home during it all, stretching out like Yogi Berra trying to beat the throw to first base, before his parents could see what hit them.

LeRoy chilled.

"I'm lazy," he said to himself, "but I'm trying to lay low."

"Excuse me, your Royal Blackness, but this is my seat," said an elderly white woman standing over his head.

LeRoy got up and changed seats.

"Sit your tired ass down," he told the woman.

"Fuck you, nigger," she said.

LeRoy raised his black fist.

"Touch me and you'll get your black ass lynched," she said. She held on tight to her patent leather purse and faked like she was going to scream.

"Beverly Hills bitch," LeRoy called her.

She spat in his face like one of the boys in the hood.

"Daisy-smellin' bitch," LeRoy called her. He looked around to make sure nobody heard him.

While it was dark outside, Rachel practiced hoodoo—

whatever that is.

She studied her welfare checks and wondered where her money had gone all these years.

"How much does it cost to go all the way to Brooklyn?" LeRoy asked the driver.

"Wiseguy, eh?" The driver pointed to a posted sign. It read: "If you wanna talk shit, be a plumber and see how far that gets you in South Central LA"

"I was only joking," said LeRoy.

"Fuck off," said the driver.

LeRoy rested himself back against the seat and cringed. He was starting to feel trapped inside of a coffin. Slivers of street lights cut across his red eyes like knives as a couple in the seats discussed suicide.

"There's no way I would do it," said the man sitting dead-behind him.

"But if you were going to, wouldn't the Golden Gate bridge be the best place?" asked a woman.

"That's what I call aspiring to great heights," the man replied. "Who'd be stupid enough to go that far?"

"You'd be surprised," said the woman.

"I sure as hell ain't Frank Sinatra," said the man. "That's for sure."

"How far is Harlem?" LeRoy asked. Clive had told him that Spike Lee's joint was in Harlem.

"That's a long way to go to get high," Bosco told Clive. He was always trying to be funny.

Clayborn ran down the cinders of an alley, dissing police left and right.

Clayborn flew through a row of garbage cans, his legs hot and peppered with ashes. His feet were chicken. He sprinted through the front and back door of a crack house, knocking over drug lords and addicts.

"Go cold turkey!" shouted a drug seller dicing crack and rock cocaine with razor blades.

A helicopter from the LAPD tracked him down.

"We got a spook," the officer radioed in.

Moving through the hood in downtown Los Angeles and past the graffiti, Clayborn saw the writing on the wall—"Cooley High" and "down with the Bloods."

Police chief Patrick White turned down his thumb and did Julius Caesar.

The coppers fired buckshot.

"They blew a hole in his muthafuckin' head big enough to carry his penis around," says one black observer.

Emotions ran wild:

1. ANGER, *The LA Sentinel,* "There is no recourse but to believe that the shooting of Clayborn Thompson was racially-motivated."

2. EXPLANATION, rap artists Public Enemy, title of album— "Fear of a Black Planet."

3. RATIONALE, LAPD chief Patrick White, "All indications were that Mr. Thompson was armed and carrying a fully-loaded gun believed to have been obtained from the crack house, just south of downtown Los Angeles."

4. LIES, LAPD, "We deeply regret what has happened."

5. GUILT, one of the participating officers, "How else can you capture a boogie?"

"None of this will ever bring my baby back," said Mrs. Thompson, dollar signs flashing inside her big head.

Rooster and Clive strode past the hospital like peacocks.

After they got to the bus stop, Rooster sat down on the bench and tore off his shoes and socks.

An old black woman strolled by, saw his feet and cracked up. "Son, you better get yourself some Epsom salts—take that swelling out."

She went on. Rooster gave her the finger behind her back.

Clive chuckled. "You got the wrong attitude," he said.

"What would you do if your feet were killing you and somebody walked by cracking jokes?" asked Rooster.

"Play it off."

"You wouldn't know any better," said Rooster.

"You crazy!"

"Who you calling crazy?"

"You, rootiepoot!"

"Funny thing I see you here right by my side," said Rooster.

"Keep looking, baby," said Clive, "cause I'm moving the crowd."

"What you announcing it for?" yelled Rooster. "You want me to hold your hand?"

"Bug off," said Clive. Then he disappeared between the trees.

LeRoy got off the bus and leaned up against the barred window of a liquor store, surrounded by houses.

The breeze of passing automobiles shook him like a doll in a dog's mouth.

The streets were born with big mouths. Parallel curbs were slick with motor oil and looked like Black lips glossed with Vasoline.

LeRoy listened for voices and wondered if he would ever escape from Compton.

Rooster stormed into Rachel's house and told her that he wanted some.

"You must be crazy!" she said. She spat a Sugar Baby into his face and laughed.

"Get the fuck out of here!" she shouted.

Rooster cackled.

She backed up two steps.

"What did you do to LeRoy?" Rooster asked.

She was thinking: "He's got your number now."

Rooster saw himself in a Little Shop of Whores.

He started singing: "Rox-anne, you don't have to play with red lights."

She backpedaled a little more.

He put on a pair of gloves.

"Rox-anne, you don't have to sell your body. You don't have to live like this."

She was thinking: "You've got to kill him somehow, or go ahead and do him."

She crept over to the corner of the room.

He got in her face, and they stood toe-to-toe.

She was sweating real hard.

He snatched her breasts and discovered how greasy-slick her chest was.

He threw her a towel.

"When I get through, you won't be able to walk," he said.

Someone came up to the door.

They heard the bell sound.

She spat into a nearby bucket, waving her fist and begging for the man to come on.

He slapped her, and they got down.

It was Sugar vs. The Hitman.

With a right hand, he knocked her down.

She kicked him, and he fell backwards into a neutral corner.

She grabbed the cord of the telephone and threatened to use it.

Ding, ding. The bell sounded again.

He rushed out of the corner and hit her with a left hook.

She spat blood, which hit his face and dripped like hot caramel.

He tore off her panties and stuck her with his thang.

She wiggled underneath—screwed herself—and raised the receiver above his big head.

He looked up and saw it.

"Girl, if you sling it," he said, "I'll damn sho' bang it!"

"Fuck you," she said. Then he slew her with a butcher knife.

"Whore!" he said. "All you was a good-for-nothin' whore!"

He flew out the door with his feet agitated and cherry-red and a trail of errors and bloody Sugar Babies left behind on the floor.

Although this is a fictional story, there is a New Jack City in every major metropolis in this country.

The Bloods And The Crips,
Starring Billy Bugle Boy

IMAGINE THE SCENE SET, Billy Bugle and a group of gangbangers like Boyz in the Hood saying "This Beat Is Hot." They're in Compton. Luther is singing "A House Is Not a Home" on compact disc. Outside, Hollywood is filming another blaxploitation movie. The producers are looking for garbage cans to make the street scenes appear authentic. Barry Michael Cooper adds the music score. Queen Latifah brings along Troop and Levert to help kick the ballistics. Chris Rock is practicing his lines and doing his make-up to look drugged out. Latifah/Troop/Levert sample "Living For The City." They do a mellow medley by the trash cans. The backdrop is Black buttered soul, Billy Bugle Boy blowing his trumpet.

"Let it go," Billy's boys said.

Billy looked at himself in the mirror, Paramount setting up cameras outside his open window.

Billy smelled revenge.

"I'm talkin' blood!" screamed Billy. "Real blood!"

Billy turned off the lights in his living room. The kid in him was gone; he lost it that day when he played Monopoly and was tossed in jail.

Revenge was now playing; it slapped Billy in the face. "Wake up, baby," it said. "I got shit to tell and a looking glass for Alice."

"You mean Alexander, don't you? He conquered most of the world known in his time."

"The difference between greatness and jive things that be is incredibly small," said Revenge. "Blood and broken bones are great. Banned AIDS and casts are jive, while Revenge is Sir-fiction and sweet."

Billy sat down and listened to a theory of rapid fire, giving himself a coke stare in the mirror. The other boys, full of caffeine in their bodies, were like The Five Heartbeats.

Billy read a sample of the *LA Sentinel* aloud: "Prostitute...butcher knife...a slew of Sugar Babies all over the floor."

Billy blew his plastic bugle. "Unfaithful people everywhere," he said to himself.

"Let it go," said the boys. "Why would anybody want to take out a two-bit whore?"

"Simple," said Billy. He was holding a can of Pepsi in his hand.

"Don't get personal!" snapped Seemo. He wasn't about to take any gump from a so-and-so self-proclaimed homicide officer who had done the nasty with a white girl.

"Cut the crap and lock the doors behind you," said Billy with a cock-of-the-walk stride. "I'm going vice and hitting the streets to find the motherfucker who killed Flip's momma." Billy moved the crowd. It was like he was caught-up in a whore-ah flick or something, black faces all around him, people preparing themselves for a B-movie.

The Bloods And The Crips,
starring Kevin Bacon as "Dopehead Jinkins,"
the negro informer.

"Dopehead," shouted Billy. "Why you dissin' me?"

The streets were full of trash, and Dopehead leaned up against the cracked glass door of an old phone booth, pulled out a bomb and lit up.

"Hey man, what's your problem? Why you calling me out?"

Billy kicked over a wino and stepped closer. Dopehead watched

suspiciously, hanging loose and shaking his booty like a jitterbug.
"How you been, Dopehead?"
Dopehead started to talk but a tooth fell out of his mouth. A
bloody needle slipped through his underwear and dropped on the
ground.
"I'm hangin'."
"What about the needle?" asked Billy.
"You want it?" asked Dopehead. He pulled out a pack of Kools
and switched them over to his other pants pocket.
"Why don't you watch where the fuck you going?" said some-
body. The story has unisex elements.
"Go fuck yourself!" shouted Billy.
Those words were like music to Dopehead: he reached down
and grabbed his thang, standing in Muddy Waters.
"It's been a long time," said Dopehead. His hair blew like fuzz
and in the dusty skies.
"The world is for niggers," said Dopehead, his gums bleeding.
"Let it go."
Billy put on the brakes. Dopehead seemed to have the jitters.
Billy approached him with caution. Dopehead was dressed like
a caution sign. Billy steered himself off to the right side of the
street.
"I got no beef with you, Dopehead," said Billy, "but I want the
son-of-a-bitch who fucked and kilt Flip's momma and put her in
ice. Where is he?"
Dopehead lowered his big head, kneeled to pick up a rusted
muffler and held it like a baby in his hands. Billy crept a bit closer
to him and then stood beside him.
"What you got?" Billy asked.
Dopehead reared his head back and switched over to a flashback:
He remembered the days when he was a part-time mechanic at
Meineke. Or was it Midas? Or was it Mr. Tune? Anyway, wherever he
was, all he ever talked about was Cadillac converters and pipe. His
work with pipe paid off when he was awarded the honor of
"Repairman of the Week." The noise of a banged-up truck-size body

with large headlights provided him with sweet memories.

Dopehead leaned farther back against the glass and smiled until parts of the door shattered from the weight of his head and brought him back to reality.

"I ain't got nothing," he said.

"What about the needle, Dopehead?"

"Oh, yeah. Somebody said it's what you call a phallic-thang." Dopehead chuckled.

"Why you carrying it around?"

"Never know when I'm in the mood to stick a red pin cushion, chee, chee."

"You goofy, Dopehead. Goofy enough to shoot gravy in your veins."

"You can't be too careful with this AIDS thang goin' round," said Dopehead. He meant "around" but the joint in his mouth cut down on the amount of syllables he was able to get out.

"You ain't got nothing to worry about, Dopehead. I ain't ever heard of a Black man catching AIDS." [Language theorist Walter J. Ong asserts that Blacks come from a primarily oral culture.]

"How would you know?" asked Dopehead. "This ain't *Marcus Welby*."

"I know cause I watch television all the time and I can tell you that it's white women like Liz'beth Taylor who worry about AIDS."

Dopehead raised his brows: "Liz'beth Taylor. Ain't that the slut that LeRoi Jones talks about?"

Dopehead stared at Billy. Like he knew poetry or something.

"I don't know, but I hate her fat ass!" said Billy. "She's the one with the big titties who's always playin' the role of some white goddess and layin' around with that other guy. She's so hincty and seddity that the next thing you know she'll be trying to make her own perfume or bottle her own stink, chee, chee."

"She makes me sick," said Dopehead. "Everytime I see her, she's in the *Enquirer*. She can't be all that. I'm as much of a freak as she is." Dopehead cracked up, white powder flying everywhere.

"You're freakier," said Billy. "You gonna help me or not?"

Dopehead blew a smoke-screen in Billy's face: "It's getting dark," he said. "I gotta go."

Billy grabbed his arm. "First, tell me where he is."

"What are you, a faggot?"

Billy glanced at Dopehead's shoes and then let go of his arm. "I gotta go," he said.

Dopehead threw the muffler down and gave him what he wanted.

"Peep the corner of Tambourine and Alameda, I think it is. Look for 'Faces'."

The phone rang, but Billy was off and running. He looked back from the alley, Dopehead looking like Handiman standing in the booth. He was a faded boogie.

The Bloods And The Crips
starring Shawana Clemons as "Yolanda Bates,"
Billy's main squeeze.

She had a room of her own. Imagine a mulatto woman with mustard for skin and pumpkins for breasts having a room of her own. It was a polyhedron with windows of cut glass and congruent polygons as bases and parallelograms as sides. Her brass bed sat in a diagonal across the room, the two posts forming right angles up against the box spring. He caressed her black skin, his fingers retracing charcoal curves like dull pencils. They lay in bed together like figures in Neoclassicism, their cold bodies partially-covered by gray drapery, their elbows and knees ashy, her right breast seemingly missing. He drew himself closer to her, their hips like two semi-circles touching each other at a single point. She stared at the chandelier, the crystal looking like a slew of ovaries or eggs tied around a Black man's neck. Gee whiz, Chandelier. She thought of calling herself Chandelier once when she was little. But back then, she was momma's crystal.

"Did you make love to me because you love me or you wanted some?" she asked.

He kissed her lips like Miles playing with his favorite instrument, his eyes fixed upon the dark brass.

"You know I love you," he said. His words were like an echo inside the Trojan Horse or from a penny hitting the floor.

"Do I?" she asked. She had a lot of nerve.

He looked at her like let-me-do-my-thang.

"Look, Billy," she said. "I'm sick and tired of all your lies. I've heard this shit before. You love me; you love me. But you come, and you don't smile or talk or show any sensitivity to how I feel. What is it you want from me, Billy?"

She turned sideways and stared at him.

"O man," he said to himself. She called him out. He raised his black glove and threatened to give her a sound, open-handed slap in the mouth.

"I need more water," said Billy. "We're doing a love scene here."

Yolanda squirted water on Billy's face and chest.

"We through," said Billy. He got out of the bed and zipped up his pants.

"Yeah, yeah, that's the story of your life," snapped Yolanda, sounding like Salt-and-Pepa. She had a sharp tongue and a smile made of cheese.

"If you so unhappy, why you let me fuck you then?"

"I thought I was different," she said.

"You are," he said. "No piece of pussy is the same."

Yolanda liked to have had a baby.

"Get out of here!" she shouted. Then she cussed him out.

He walked a straight line to the door, opened it and then turned back around.

"I'm sorry," he said. "I didn't mean to say that."

"Close the door behind you, nigger," she said.

He slammed the door and hesitated in the hallway.

"Let it go," he remembered his boys saying. He took off half-naked in broad daylight and with the song "Good Morning, Heartache" on his mind. Or was it "Goodbye, Heartache?"

She heard him go down the steps as the phone rang.

He hit the emergency exit when he heard her say "hello."
She answered the phone feeling like she would never kiss him
again. That's why he left; she had given him some French and
sliced him to pieces.

The Bloods And The Crips,
starring NBA Sacramento Kings' forward Lionel Simmons
as "Lionel 'Little Train' Taylor"
and world heavyweight boxing ex-champ Leon Spinks
as "Leon Jackson."

Faces stood at the center of Ten City. It was a raggedy-looking
nightclub on the Southside of Los Angeles, but, inside, it featured
Kool jazz sets and a dance floor. Billy strolled in late like he was
the stuff.

"Give me a heavy-wet on the rocks," he said to Joe, the
bartender.

Black people turned around in their seats and stared.

You know how niggaz are; they made him a star.

Joe came back with his drink and handed it to him. Billy saw
the ice cubes dance in the alcohol like skinny-dippers playing in
the surface water of a pool. He shot a glance at the glass, then slid
the drink back to the bartender.

"Take it back," he said.

"What's wrong with it?" asked Joe. He gave Billy the evil eye.

"I wanted some real rocks," he said, "like diamonds." Luckily,
he said it to himself.

Joe looked at Billy like he had a problem, then took his little
money and stepped over to the other side of the bar: "Who's next?"
he asked.

Billy pulled up a chair and positioned himself near the center
aisle. He felt hurt and worn out. He studied couples walking as
he stuffed his identification back into his pants pocket. Trashy-
looking white dames with cigarettes in their hands watched and
smiled as he dug into his pants.

The Bloods And The Crips,
introducing Missy White as filler.

He did the cha-cha with one of the white women and then took her upstairs and fucked her in the closet. She had thin lips, large pink nipples and a little ass. He tore her booty up. She seemed barely able to walk by the time he was through. She was glad, however, that he didn't use a condom.

He let her walk out of the closet first. He followed a couple minutes later. When he got back to the bar downstairs, she called him on it: "This man raped me," she said.

What did she say that for? Negroes started tripping out.

"How was it?" asked Joe.

"If you through with it, let us have some too."

"Negro, you ought to be ashamed of yourself. She's the town slut."

"What you got against brown meat?"

"Next time, take that shit to the crib."

Negroes formed coalitions:

"Most of us ain't never had a white woman before."

"I don't see why not."

"You can get one anytime."

"They come a dime a dozen."

"Well, at least they don't be actin' funny about giving it up."

"How you know?" a woman asked the man sitting besides her.

He tried to play her off. "Don't worry about how I know," he said.

She got up and tried to split, but he snatched her black ass back to the table. "Where the fuck you think you going, bitch?"

She called him a black m.f. and tossed a glass of Old Tom in his face. A fight broke out.

Meantime, the white woman kept shouting "Rape!"

Billy cracked up. "You in Compton, baby," he said. "Who cares?"

Billy leaned back and listened to house music, people bumping up against him. He was bleeding on the chair, still hurt, thanks to that cutting incident he had with Shawana at the end of the love scene. He refused to call her "Yolanda" because she was a bad actress. Once, she almost killed him during a biting love scene. Billy sat bleeding on the chair. The crowd hollered and screamed. A fine cigarette woman selling Kool on colored people's time tip-toed into the corner of the room and laughed, money all down in her cleavage as if it were a ticket box. Billy tapped his fingers on the edge of the wooden chair.

The Bloods And The Crips,
starring Lionel Simmons and Leon Jackson.

Billy was bleeding, thanks to that no-good dum-ass Black bitch Shawana, who once played a whore in *Scarface*. He refused to fuck her again. It was that simple. He was tired of compromising.

He glared at the entrance.

The Bloods And The Crips,
starring two brothers who ain't gonna get paid
if they don't get their Black asses out here.

Billy was bleeding, thanks to that stupid-ass Shawana, who must've left her script at the crib. She wasn't supposed to cuss him out like that. But he played it off, which will probably prove confusing but no big deal. This whole thang was making no sense anyway.

Billy wished that he was in the director's chair. After all, everythang was out of control.

He glared towards the entrance.

The Bloods And The Crips,
starring Mr. Firkusny as a dude in Billy's hood.

"I'm the one you're looking for."

"Who the hell are you?" asked Billy. "And why are you whispering over my shoulder?"

"I'm Mr. Firkusny, and I'm white."

"So, what you want me to do about it?"

"I want you to end all of this colored shit and go back to black-and-white, so I can resume playing the piano at my leisure and forget about all of this house music and shit." The traditional idea is that Mr. Firkusny—pronounced FIRKUSE-NEE—can say anything he wants to because he's white.

Billy looked the other way. "I can't." He paused. "You see, I'm in too deep."

"This whole thang is over basketball shoes, isn't it? Money, it's gotta be da shoes." Mr. Firkusny was trying to talk Black.

"Yep."

"And Rooster. This goes way back, doesn't it?"

"Yep."

"The whore. How does the whore figure in?"

"She was Flip's momma."

"But, I thought Flip was a Blood."

"Yep."

"Then why would Rooster dust her?"

"Maybe he hates dirt. I don't know. What you asking me for? You pop in here out of nowhere and expect me to buy some singsong about you being the one to talk to. Who you think I am?"

"I know who you are," said Mr. Firkusny. "Look at you. You holding your stomach and bleeding. You're a crip."

"If you know all this, why you here?"

"The guys who originally were supposed to be here couldn't make it. They got picked up in Watts or Irwindale or Inglewood or nearby Crenshaw or somewhere after trying to hold up a liquor store with a Betty Crocker knife."

"Couldn't they do better than that?"

"One of them had a frozen stick of margarine."

"Go on."

"When the cops stopped them, they tried to argue that their stocking masks were wave caps."

"Go on."

"They were busted after the police pulled off their masks and saw that their heads were still nappy."

"That's a trip," said Billy. "What, did they think that robbery was a piece of cake or something?" Mr. Firkusny chuckled but looked confused.

"I mean, that's a wild story, considering nobody got iced."

"Yes, it is. But even more obstreperous than that is the fact that they were wearing British Knights when they got incarcerated." Mr. Firkusny was regressing a bit.

"What the hell was they doing wearing British Knights? They must have been desperate for a pair of shoes."

"Yes, well, reportedly, they held up a couple of unsuspecting wayfarers en route to what you people call the juice house." Mr. Firkusny was really struggling to throw out some Black dialogue.

"You talk like you got a paper ass," said Billy.

"Give me a break," said Mr. Firkusny. "I am a cardboard character. What did you expect to find at such a short notice? Liberace?"

"I walked in late, though. You should have had your act together."

Mr. Firkusny blew on his cigar, eyeing Billy's sneakers. "This whole thang is over basketball shoes, isn't it?"

"Yes. But don't forget the drugs. It's all about drugs, too."

"And gangs, Billy. Don't forget the gangs."

"Yes, Compton is full of bloods and crips. But what I can't figure out is, what you doin' in the middle of all this?"

"Simple."

"Lay off that!" said Billy.

"Sorry."

"You fly. Go on with your story, old man."

Mr. Firkusny ushered Billy back into the other room and spoke during the performance of a live band.

The Bloods And The Crips,
special guest appearance by Mojo Stew.

Mojo had snare drums, did jazz and sang the blues.

"Listen to me," said Mr. Firkusny. "We're in a nightclub with

Compton's most wanted. Nobody cares about us. The big picture is not about what you think it is. It's like somebody had reversed the script. Some Black s.o.b. is pulling strings for himself and mum is the word."

"Straight up?"

"Dead serious," said Mr. Firkusny. "Can't you tell that this whole thang doesn't make sense?"

"Yes, because I don't understand what a white man is doing in the middle of a Black struggle."

"I was dragged in here as a last-minute substitute. Originally, Lionel and Leon were going to talk you. They would have spoken well on the subject of house music. But, when things got tight, I was brought in here to entertain the crowd with the piano."

"Yes, house music is full of piano."

"I have no clue what house music is, but with a nigger flicker at my back I played for hours until you came. You're being set up, Billy. And I'm being used."

Mr. Firkusny rolled up the sleeves of his white dinner jacket and showed Billy his fingertips. They were all taped with Band-Aids.

"Serves you right," said Billy.

Mr. Firkusny, his gold cuff links ripped off his sleeves, walked Billy back out into the main room, where he was immediately snatched and forced to resume playing the piano.

"We're all puppets, Billy. But house music can't last forever."

Mr. Firkusny slumped over the keyboard and played house music.

"True. But you'll be dead—before it quits."

Billy straightened Mr. Firkusny's bow tie and then strolled out the door.

"You're never too young to die!" yelled Mr. Firkusny.

But Billy had already left.

He was standing on the street corner like a rusty sign warning people of a dead inn.

Meantime, the phone rang several times inside Faces but DJ Farley Grandmaster Funk was flipping the tracks with London house and nobody thought the ring was from the telephone.

The Bloods And The Crips,
starring Petra Blakeman-Harrison as Billy's rich mistress.

"Get away from my man!" yelled Yolanda.

"Get away from my face!" screamed Petra.

"Get away from my apartment!"

"Get away from my purse!" The Bloods And The Crips

"Get away from my undergarments, you skinny, little-ass, flat-chested slut!"

"Get away from my lotion, you Black-ashy bitch!"

"Get away from my protein!" Yolanda puckered her lips.

Petra confessed to filling her lips with gelatin.

"Get away from my big-tooth plastic comb!" Petra screamed.

Yolanda felt her hair, peeped Petra's royal blue panties.

"Quit screwing my man or I'm going to tell your parents what you've been doing with your money."

Petra froze. "How did you find out?"

"Billy went to the barber and had the initials 'PB' cut into the side of his hair. But after he took off his shoes to make love to me, I saw the same initials written in crayon on his leather uppers after bending over the bed to smell his feet. He told me that his feet were not funky and that the initials meant 'Pretty Basketball,' but ain't nobody stupid enough to believe that Billy can afford his own pair of Air Jordan's. I knew that some white bitch was buying him shoes. Now get out of my apartment!"

"Well, I never!"

"You should try. Then, maybe, you wouldn't have such a big gap between your legs, you sleazy Nigger-lover! Stanky piece of white trash!"

Petra waltzed outside and into the hallway. Yolanda slammed the door behind her.

"Nigger!" screamed Petra. Then she boogied away, jiggling her pearls on the way to find the Black man responsible.

Billy felt like a hitchhiker at a stop sign, which seemed to be the story of his life.

Billy fell asleep with his head up against a pink octagon and a collection of muddled voices talking smack to him. He saw James Brown, "The Godfather of Soul," Ned "The Wino," Natalie Cole, Little Richard and Madonna with those two pointed metal cups over her breasts. James Brown was inside his body trying to repair the damage that had been done. (Imagine internal bleeding.) Ned "The Wino" was trying to go back to Good Times. Natalie Cole was singing "Unforgettable." Billy could see her beautiful dark skin clinging like mud to a white dress, her nipples like chunks of peat squirted with lighter fluid. Little Richard was playing the piano, shaking his head and spraying everyone with Sta-Sof from his curl. Before they all went to work, Madonna got them all together and they said a prayer. Then she went on a stabbing spree with her pointers, ripping out his heart and guts like they were nothing.

Ned "The Wino" clogged Billy's veins with bottles. And Billy, while he was out of it, was having problems breathing. In his sleep, he wondered if Rooster had any of these problems: Here was a man who killed a woman but never slowed down long enough to think about it. It was strange how life hurt the people who didn't deserve it and how people hurt themselves. There was no consistency to it. There was only Madonna with two pointers and blood by her nipples.

Billy woke up standing erect at the stop sign, some ugly m.f. moving up-and-down in front of his face and pointing his finger while eating out of a bowl of yellow popcorn.

"I'm your worse nightmare," said the person.

"No, Madonna is," Billy replied.

The Black gangbanger standing up in Billy's face looked confused.

"Are we playing Truth or Dare?" the blood asked.

"We always been playing it," said Billy.

"You playing the nutroll," blood said. He pulled out a home-made knife and aimed it toward Billy's face.

Still bleeding, Billy staggered back up against the stop sign and slumped over, barely able to do anything, his plastic bugle underneath his feet.

"You a crip," said blood. He carefully approached with the knife, pieces of masking tape dangling on the handle.

"Don't do it," said Billy. "You just a teenage boy."

Blood stopped in his tracks. "Holdup," he said. "I keep getting dirt on my shoes." He had on a pair of Pumps by Reebok and was tiptoeing so he wouldn't get them dirty.

"How do you work those?" asked Billy.

"You talking about these shoes?"

"Yes."

"See this lever on the side. You just pump up and air out."

"Good—that's damn good," Billy muttered.

"Yeah, that's the reason I can't put my foot in your ass," said blood.

Billy was shocked by the profanity. No censorship. It was like God or the almighty Creator had fallen asleep too and let thangs go to hell.

"They expensive?"

"Naw. Not if you're makin' cash money."

"You got a slight British accent," said Billy. Then it hit him: "Those shoes! That gold rope and oversize clock around your neck! That voice! You're Doug E. Fresh, notorious neighborhood king of rap music!"

"Who was you expectin'? Gil-Scott Heron?"

"What makes you think I was lookin' for you?"

"It doesn't matter," said Doug E. "I wasn't looking for you. But you invaded my territory. You had no business being here. You should have just walked away. Dig?"

"Mr. Rap-king, I'd appreciate it if you would get your greasy fingers out of my face."

"Hey man, that's real butter!"

"Who cares, baby?"

Billy shoved Doug E. with an elbow and proceeded to walk away.

"Hey man, you stepped on my shoe." Doug E. seemed shocked. "What did you step on my shoe for?"

Billy backed up.

"I'm gonna kick your ass!" yelled Doug E.

"Somebody call for help!" Billy screamed. "Call Yolanda! Call my girlfriend! Call anybody!"

The Bloods And The Crips,
featuring a beautiful Black woman
as the Soul Connection.

Yolanda has dialed 1-900-FOR-SOUL a lot of times, but this is the longest she's ever talked:

"Girl, you know that bitch had the nerve to come over. I'm not kidding, girl. I couldn't believe it. I tripped. Yes, girl. She gone come over here and start talkin' about how I fucked her man. She can have the nigger for all I care. I don't want 'im no way. I'm going to hook up with someone who'll take care of me. Billy is a trip. He's insecure with himself and too caught up in acting Black. What? I know that's right, girl. I betta let you go. It's two-fifty for the first minute and we've been on the phone almost a hour. I'll talk to you later. I've got some reading to do anyway."

"It's over for you, punk! You should have taken those Nike Air Jordans on your feet and used them to fly away!"

"Damn it, Fresh! Don't do it!" cried Billy.

"Sorry, punk. There ain't enough room for both of us." (Rappers use more cliches than anyone.)

"On your knees, punk!"

Black people came out of their houses and watched from a distance, but no one made a move to stop it. A phone in a nearby booth rang, but everyone, except Dopehead, was too busy trying to see what was going to happen.

"God bless the child," an elderly neighborhood woman whispered.

"Children are like clay," whispered another woman. "It all

depends on who's hands they're put in."

"Damn it, man—I'm sorry!"

"Quit cryin'."

Doug E. was about to do him when suddenly he stopped. "Say, don't I know you from somewhere? Yo' face looks familiar. What was you doing around here anyway?"

"Flip was my boy," said Billy, crying. "I had to know the truth."

"The fact that often people don't get what they deserve—or, sometimes, get what they didn't deserve—makes you miserable, doesn't it? You can't be happy until you know the reason why, right?"

"Yes."

"Let me see if I can help: The dude who did Flip's momma. I saw him out in the street that day. My man was very unstable. I tried to get him to chill out, but he wouldn't listen to me. He had pussy on his mind. He took off and ran away during the middle of a rumble. I tried to stop him, but she was already fucked by the time I got there."

Billy wailed. All of the people watching remained expressionless.

Doug E. plunged the knife into's Billy's Adam's apple.

"You're Billy Holiday!" he yelled. "You doomed to sing the blues forever!"

Dopehead, a rather ominous man, staggered out of the crowd and shouted: "Hey Billy, that was your momma on the phone. She said to cut out all the gangshit and get yo' ass home. She said it's time to eat and the Bulls are on TV. She been looking for you all day."

In a quick drive-by shooting, Rooster hit Billy twice and nicked Doug E. and dropped him. Dopehead stood and watched.

"Villains are...people whose daring and energy of character might have made them heroes in a better-organized society."

—*The Los Angeles Times*

Doing The Nasty With
A Nigger Flicker & Slashing Rain

I<small>T IS NOT A GOOD NIGHT</small> to be Clive. Rooster climbed the winding stair of a chocolate building in Compton with blood on his feet and the wooden door of apartment 3G hiding in the dark hallway like the insides of a television set. When the pitter-patter restarted, Rooster was on his tiptoes, sneaking around on a floor of hot picture tubes, glass and shit stinging the bottom of his heel, a wino watching him through a bottle of warm Canadian Mist, melted nougat stuck to the sole of his feet. Blackout.

It was very spooky, Rooster says. He is washing his big black hands and feet in the basin, wiping the blood away. He is talking about mommas and bent trees and funky storms and water babies falling and busting their heads on the sidewalk, heroin and crack cocaine everywhere. He's got a box of candy stuffed inside his drawers like a price tag and cuts all over himself. He's got nicks and grooves on the side of his big head from living on the edge.

Where you been, I ask him. (My lipstick is smeared.)

On a motherfucking trip, he replies.

I bet you have, I respond.

He fingers a stack of books. I see his eyes searching. He slams Stephen King's *Misery* back down on the coffee table and stares

out the open window—down to the wet sidewalk, down the
drain, down into a dive on the corner to get drunk, down into a
hole where he fucks a street prostitute with the depth of his
thoughts. He spies on her as she walks the thin line like a flat note
in a musical composition. Her pimp is pointing at her, singing
"Teddy's Jam." She pops Juicy Fruit, chewing gum, working the
strip.

She has big titties, he says, and watching her enlarges his brain.
(My little girl runs away.)
What's wrong, baby?
He tells me his story.
An auto wreck on Alameda Street, he says. A terrible accident.
Blood everywhere. Ambulances descending on the scene like
crows. Puddles of blood like apples smashed on the street. People
hollering everywhere, a Black market. A Rolls-Royce rammed into
a tree. The ignition keys clean out in the middle of the street.
Everybody screaming at a scarecrow hanging on the hubcap of a
sewer hole, skin all around and all over the pavement like straw.
Women gagging, spit coming out like weed-killer. Stevie Wonder
at the corner.

Real surreal shit, I tell him. But what does it mean?
Somebody got fucked in a hit-and-run experience, he answers.
Who got banged up? I ask him. Who got banged up?
(He pauses.)
A woman, I think. (He is erect when he talks to me.) I heard she
was already knocked up before she got banged again.
Did she have on clean underwear, I ask.
I'm not sure, he replies.
Then, who did it, I ask. Who did it?
He looks out the window, where the lights blink and snakes
crawl on the tarred pavement.
Black out.

Downed wires flood the street outside my apartment building.
When I look out and down below, I see palm trees with perms.

I see Maple with a wet curl in her hair and sparks playing in it like struck matches. The leaves shake like barrettes. My bottom lip touches the taste of dew drops as it hangs out over the ledge. No rain now. Water droplets rest on the Kool surface, loose cigarettes scattered all around the area. I cannot see it, but I know there is a rainbow; it smells like raspberry-lime-orange sherbet as the air grows colder.

Get out of the window, he says. Somebody might see you.
   I sit down on the bed and write with a No. 2 pencil and pad.
   What's going on, I ask him.
   He walks over, gazing at my scribble.
   The lines are down, he says.
   How about the telephones?
   The telephones are down, too, he answers. People are calling each other with empty tin cans from greens.
   Nervous, I pinch the vein in his arm.
   Can't squeeze blood out of a turnip, I tell him.
   He cracks up.
   Blackout.
   The lights are blinking and it is driving us crazy.
   What's going on, I ask him.
   He puts his hand over the lamp-shade and taps it. As the lamp shakes, black and white alternate in the room like piano keys, his fingers playing death knocking on the door.
   There is the smell of more rain coming. Rooster sticks his big head back out the window to see what's happening.
   You can't stop the rain, he says.
   Loose Ends.
   How does it look outside? I ask Rooster.
   Black out, he says. His voice trickles through the room.
   C'mere, baby, I whisper.
   He pulls his head out of the window, turns and stares.
   What? he asks.
   I was talking to my little girl.

You trippin', he says.

What you mean, I ask him.

She as big as a house and you got the nerve to be calling her a baby!

He picks up another book and reads inside.

Get out of my apartment!

He seems stunned. He points to the text in his hands.

Read this and tell me what you think, he says. It is a short story. Clive's name is penciled on the first page.

What is this shit, he asks.

Why don't you tell me, I reply.

He circles the room, Sugar Babies dropping out of his underwear. He stomps them, squishing caramel in his own face.

You killing them, I try to tell him.

Big deal, he answers.

He is a cold muthafucker and his hands are still wet. He touches my nipples with ice water.

He's got a nigger flicker inside the elastic trim on his white briefs and is ready to do the nasty. He touches my nipples with ice.

I lie down on the bed and push down my panties, my baby hiding in the bathroom.

He grins and then drops his underwear and knife.

We fuck and cuss and bang each other like cymbals crashing. He tries to tear me up so I would holler. He slaps me harder and harder on the edge, spreading my legs over the end of the bed and raising them toward the ceiling fan with the caked palm of his hands.

Sometimes I cry. He fucks me while I smell the rain coming, but it is too late. I scream for him to stop.

He strikes me like lighting, wiggling his black ass faster as it lays on top of me.

Slow drops. Then, everything all at once.

He did me good. But I asked for it.

You can fuck yo' ass off, he says. He seems charged with energy. He moves through the room with no clothes on, semen dripping on the floor.

We are talking weird shit here.

I can't fuckin' explain it.

Do you see my candy bar, Rooster asks.

Describe it, I demand.

It's a long, thick piece of hard dark chocolate...peanuts, he answers.

Shit-t-t.

I crawl out of the bed with bare feet and tiptoe on the wet floor. Rooster says that he will not leave without his chocolate, so I lean over to check underneath the coffee table—desperately looking for Mr. Goodbar.

He watches my nipples droop like bullets as I reach down while the breeze from the window shoots through the room, blowing wrappers away and penetrating my undergarments. The storm tries to fuck me again.

Take your candy and get the hell out of here! I yell.

I feel moist air shooting between my legs as I bend over, Rooster refusing to let me close the window.

"Quit!" I scream.

I take his chocolate and order him to put it into the shorts on the floor, but he just keeps pushing me.

Take it! he insists. Your daughter has put her mouth on it!

Why are you going off, I ask him. It's just a little piece of chocolate.

An Almond Joy! he shouts.

A Mound, I say nonchalantly. A Baby Ruth, A Butterfinger, A Whatchamacallit.

Don't fuck with me! Rooster shouts.

Rooster is clientele so I try to understand him. Our relationship is based upon reciprocation: He empties his bank for me, and I give him what he wants. We do it behind Clive's back.

Rooster is disturbed on the inside. He shows me the book again and asks if I have read it.

I hope to be reading my own book one day, I tell him.

He snatches the pad of paper and looks at my scribble again.

You better learn how to use quotations before you go out and try to sell this shit, he says.

He tosses the pad out the window.

What's your problem, I ask him.

How am I supposed to know, he asks. You're the expert on men. Why don't you tell me?

(He wants me to play doctor.)

We live in a throw-away society, I tell him, and when we throw away things it hurts the people who are associated with them.

He lies down on the couch, hanging his knees out over the arm, expecting more.

I grab my pencil and another pad and sit on the bed next to him and the book on his stomach.

He points to my vagina with his index finger but is looking at the walls around him.

You've got big-ass-room here, he says.

He talks to me like I'm a whore.

While he reads aloud, I rewrite the beginning of my book:

IT WAS BLACK MONDAY WHEN ROOSTER CAME TO ME LIKE A STORM. HE WAS MAD, HIS MIND STUCK IN SEX. IT RAINED ALL NIGHT. ROOSTER CLAIMED HE SAW A TWO-CAR ACCIDENT. ONE PERSON WAS KILLED, HE SAYS. I LET HIM GET IT OUT OF HABIT AND BECAUSE I DIDN'T KNOW WHAT ELSE TO DO.

No good, I mumble. I tear off the first sheet and throw it into the waste basket.

Second draft. Alcohol by my side.

THE DISTANT RAIN SMELLS LIKE A LOVER, WOMEN IN HAITI WITH WOVEN BASKETS OVER THEIR HEADS—CARRYING LOADS OF PRECIPITATION.

Come back to Jamaica, I remember a commercial on television saying.

I make a paper wad and lay it on the table. I ain't ready for that story yet.

What the hell are you doing, Rooster asks. I'm talkin' to you.

What do you want, Rooster?

He is never satisfied.

This story, with Clive penciled on the first page, has my girlfriend's name in it, he says.

And what name is that, I ask lackadaisically.

Diana, he says. You know that my girlfriend's name is Diana! You act like you're jealous!

Dirty Diana? Jealous of that black, skinny-ass bitch? Don't kid yourself. I got all I want from you.

You got nothin', Rooster screams.

Don't ever think that there's something between us, I tell Rooster, cause there isn't. You're just a little Black man shaking your booty...

All night long, says Rooster before I can finish.

I grab a bottle of alcohol off the table and get sloppy with a drink. He's right. When I look around, I see nothing: a couch with stains, a lamp-shade designed by Fingers anonymous, a thin dark closet with an empty belly, et cetera.

Snap out of it, bitch, Rooster yells. You ain't in Kansas!

He cackles, stretching out below a hanging wall plaque that reads Home Sweet Home. Then he thumbs through a rack of record albums.

I love Janet Jackson, he exclaims. Remember her from Good Times? She's got big titties, and she's been showing more and more of them lately.

So what's your point, I ask him.

He looks at his thang and puts his underwear back on.

I refill the glass with alcohol and set it on the coffee table. Shots of warm liquor drop down my throat like wounded swallows while I write some more.

I AM WISHING THAT ROOSTER WOULD TOUCH IN THE MORNING AND LET THAT BE HIS COUPE DE GRACE. WHAT WE'RE DOIN' IS WRONG. BUT, IT'S THE ONLY THING ROOSTER KNOWS HOW TO DO.

He gazes out into the blue rain. The rain is falling notes in a sad song—So Many Tears by Billie Holiday.

Play misty for me, Rooster begs. He's got a fistful of dollars in his black hand and is looking at me like I would do it for a few dollars more.

What the hell are you talking about, I ask him. He has never asked me to play misty for him before.

Tell me again what happened between you and Clive, he demands.

As I speak, he places the nigger flicker and wad of money on the arm of the couch:

It was a night similar to this when Clive rode into town on his dogie and swept me off my feet, I tell Rooster. He [Clive] was LaRue then. He was stone cold. The boy knew how to make me laugh. We talked at a bar until sunrise. Then I took him home and fucked him. He slapped me like a pair of blue jeans being washed on heavy stone. 'LaRue, you are the fastest gunslinger in the West,' I told him. 'Make it last forever.'

He couldn't, could he, Rooster asks.

Nope, I reply, Clive was embarrassed. He grabbed his dogie and galloped away.

That's too bad, says Rooster, mimicking the three-beat movement of the legendary LaRue.

Yes, it was, I remark to Rooster, because two weeks later I found out that I was carrying a load.

Was it Clive's, Rooster asks. Was it Clive's? (Rooster knows the answer but fakes like he hasn't heard the story before.)

No, it wasn't, I reply. It was from a previous relationship, but Clive thought it was his.

Did you tell him that it wasn't his sucker, Rooster asks. (He's got his feet on the couch as if my apartment were a saloon.)

I go on: I never told Clive about the baby, I answer. He thought he had fucked a virgin, not a dancing girl.

Ah, this explains your affinity for hardcore music and your disgusting sensitivity to beatings, Rooster says. When you heard the pitter-patter going on outside your door, you opened the door to see if it was Clive coming back.

Yes, nobody can do me like Clive, I answer, but he's scared. Right now, he's too afraid to come back.

It would have been nice, Rooster says, then you wouldn't have had to open the door for me.

You remind me of the story of Cain and Abel, I tell Rooster. One a lover, one a hater. What happened to the days when you and Clive were in the same gang?

This is nothing but double talk! Rooster shouts. What makes you think that Clive is ever going to come back?!

You ask a good question, Rooster. A damn good question.

I'm tired of talking about you, he says. Let's talk about me.

What do you wanna talk about, I ask.

Diana, he says. This story says that Diana has lost her marbles within the crevices of modern society.

Perhaps she intentionally dropped them, I reply, which would of course imply that they were not really lost but rather casually let go. Perhaps there are too many choices here.

Shut up cracking jokes before I slit your throat, Rooster screams.

He is trippin' trying to figure out what Diana has done with her marbles. He looks up the word crevices. "A narrow crack; fissure." This is in *American Heritage*. ("History in general is but a collection of crimes, follies, and misfortunes," according to Voltaire.) Fine definition, he says, except for one thing: He looks up the word fissure. "A narrow crack, usu. of considerable size."

Rooster looks at me and stares in whore-ah. Diana's been fuckin' with other people. Not other men. But other people. It is a common occurrence in human society, but Rooster refuses to believe that she would do it to him.

How much alcohol does it take for a woman to get drunk, he asks.

IT IS NOT A GOOD NIGHT.

I can't finish.

Rooster ignores me. He believes everything that he reads. It is obvious to him that something wild is going on.

But perhaps there are too many choices here. So he goes over a few of them. Maybe he wasn't giving her enough and left her with no choice but to find it elsewhere. Perhaps when they went to Clive-nem's party together, he lost her and she was forced to take part in a group thang. Or maybe at the same party, she lost him and got mixed up in something that was over her head.

He must decide which ones are true.

He will call her: Plan A (he wants me to write it down), he will bluntly ask her if she's fuckin with other people. If she says no, he will end it there. If she says yes, they will talk about it further over the phone. No, scratch that, he says. It's too lame. If she says yes, he will tell her to take her black ass over to his crib. That way they can discuss it face-to-face. Plan B, he will brutally fuck her until her crack widens and stays open like a V or the Grand Canyon. Wait, one choice too many here. Diss the V. He likes the Grand Canyon-analogy better.

You mean canon, don't you? (I am acting silly.)

Shut up! Rooster screams.

Whatever you want, I answer.

Get this down, Rooster tells me: Diana's booty is like the Grand Canyon and I'm going to pump it until it runs dry.

What an imagination, I say.

He grins. He likes the idea of giving it to her.

Back to Plan B. He will get it and then let Clive have her. They'll run a train on her.

He grins. He pulls a black, broken steel caboose out of his shorts.

Not the train, I tell Rooster.

Why not?

It's too terrible.

We giggle and he puts it back in his underpants.

He continues with Plan B until he finishes it. Then he wheels and stares at me.

What do you think, he asks.

How does she make you feel, I ask. (I am referring to Dirty Diana.)

He tries to describe it.

I can't put it into words.

He tries to describe it again.

When Diana and I are together, Rooster says, my heart is a singing bird.

Then call Diana and tell her you still want it, I tell Rooster.

I pick up the telephone and urge him to come and do it. He pushes me down on the bed and strips away my panties as if it were a will-o'-the-wisp blinding his eyes.

Maybe this is why your girlfriend won't fuck you, Rooster.

Rooster rises and grabs his head.

The shit has to stop, I tell Rooster.

Wait, he says.

He skates along the floor. He appears glassy-eyed while pointing his index in my face, ready to X me out.

It takes action to get action! Rooster shouts.

True, but this is not by any means necessary! I yell.

Rooster looks the other way.

Talk to me, Rooster. (When a mental patient is troubled, doctors urge the patient/victim to talk the problem out.)

Rooster decides to cooperates: I'm in a whore-ah house, he says, and a ho is trying to tell me what to do with my life. No, scratch that. If I call you a ho it makes me look bad. Plus, it sounds derogatory.

Rooster cuts the rug, picks up a couple of dusty records and throws them toward the turntable. He tries to remix his speech:

I'm in a whore-ah house and one of the women is trying to tell me what to do with my life. She's got a half-empty glass of alcohol on the coffee table. She's got a pack of Kool chilling on the side of a square ashtray, two cigarettes with rosy lipstick on their butts, another cig caught in her fingers. She scratches her leg and flicks ashes off onto the floor. Pay no attention to the people in the street shouting 'fuck it,' she says. Then she tells me that she let some of my buddies do her. This ruins it all. Now I know that her titties have been felt on.

You got metaphorical on me, I tell Rooster.

I'm blowin' up, he replies. His head is a hot air balloon that keeps rising.

Titties, Rooster. I don't like that word titties.

He looks at me like who-asked-you.

You'll have to do better than that, I tell him.

I'm the boss here—you're just a whore livin' large, he yells.

Rooster is where the wild thangs are; he gnashes his terrible teeth.

Don't try to intimidate me, I shout.

"I am strong. I am invincible. I am woman."

I am playing old music on the turntable.

Helen Ready is out, Rooster shouts. He snatches the record and tosses it out the window. People shout 'fuck you' from the street. He walks over to the window and pops his head out into the rain.

Kiss my black ass, he shouts. (This is what deviant behavior looks like—an iceberg, an ass bending over, the top sticking out where people can see it but everything else secret.)

Rooster turns back around and wonders if he said the right thing. He could have told them to go jump in a lake, but there are no lakes in Compton. Maybe it would have been better if he had yelled fuck you, too. Maybe he talks too much.

He cracks up thinking about it.

I pick up the telephone and hand it to him.

Call her and tell her that you still want it.

He dials her number. She answers the phone on the fifth ring (he was so close to hanging up). A long pause, static as if the connection is to Long Beach. Hello, Diana, he says, I can hear you breathing. I dash to the bathroom to find my baby and come back out to discover him holding the receiver against his chest and whispering. She won't talk to me, he says. Tell her you love her, I mutter. You think I'm crazy? You think I'm stupid? He gives me two very difficult questions to answer. I gaze inside my glass and search for a crystal-clear response. Meantime, he trembles like an ice cube floating in hot water. Tell her that you love her, I say. He hesitates to do it. He wants more options. She won't believe me, he argues. Your chances are slim, I admit. That's because she has a little ass, he says. She knows what you're about, Rooster. Cane (coke, cocaine), says Rooster, raisin' Cain. He puts the receiver back on his ear. I hear you breathing, Diana. Talk to me. The phone is dead, says Rooster. It is not Rooster's day. If he dies today, his epitaph will read here lies Rooster, a dumb-ass fucker. This is what he seems to be thinking.

Diana, say something or I'm going to hang up.

He frets.

Translation: The phone is dead, and Dirty Diana has gone to the funeral.

Talk to me, Rooster begs.

Speculation: Diana has buried the telephone.

(He rigs an explosive statement.)

Diana, get yo' ass on the damn phone or hang up.

Prediction: He's gonna find out why I call her Dirty Diana.

We both hear a click.

It figures she would take that option, Rooster says.

He hangs up the receiver and then dials again.

How far is Long Beach, he asks.

Ye of little faith, I reply.

(Diana answers on the second ring.)

I need you, Diana, Rooster whispers into the receiver. (I can look at his whore-id face and tell that he is talking about doing the nasty.)

He grins and pulls the caboose out of his shorts.

No, she screams. It's as if she's seen his caboose before.

He looks at me like what-the-hell-should-I-do.

Well...

There is a knock on the door.

Rooster is jumpy, awfully jumpy, wondering who it might be.

He tries to tell me all the possibilities. The cops? His daddy? Clive?

Could be, I tell him.

Which one? he asks.

All of them and throw in your momma, too, I answer.

While he ducks down to the floor, I stroll past the arm of the couch and open the door.

A sleazy-looking white woman stands in the hallway with a cigarette in her mouth.

I'm looking for the man who said kiss my black ass.

Get the fuck out of here, I whisper. Then I slam the door.

A relieved Rooster is back on the phone, talking rhetoric.

Baby, you're the only one for me, Rooster tells Dirty Diana. And then he hears another click.

Rooster looks at me like I did it.

Don't you ever talk about my momma again! he shouts.

Rooster struts over to the door and opens it.

I've gotta go, he says. I've got something else to do.

Wait! I scream to Rooster. I've got something to give you!

I waltz over to Rooster and give him a few Kisses—then slice the side of his belly with his own nigger flicker. I push him out of the door and into the dark hallway. With the door of apartment 3G closed and locked, I hear Rooster run away, tapping the boards under his feet like rain.

I look out the window and down to the street to find him. In nothing but an off-white pair of Fruit-Of-The-Loom, Rooster looks like a partially-deflated automobile tire bouncing on the pavement. He plays hopscotch in reggae-splash along the sidewalk, graffiti and shit under his feet.

He sees me in the window.

One, two, three, crack! Rooster yells. One, two, three, crack!

He runs over a garbage can and straight down Alameda Street, where children jump rope and repairmen are everywhere.

More Mental

ROOSTER QUIETLY SAT on somebody's stoop watching Yolanda she hit the steps looking up cotton above her big head LeRoi Jones' or Amiri Baraka's *The Slave* in her black hands. She wore embryonic eyes and a flower dress Drop waist out on the porch late night as repairmen came by and smiled with snakes crawling near her feet Then they threw cable off their shoulders like it was chain or thread for stitches and went to work in front of her. Rooster bled under a tree chomping candy hard and noisily Tuning out the world switching back and forth between present and Past a bottle of Campho Phenique for infection.

Rubber repairman Rubber repairman Rubber repairman. Rooster realized that one of the repairmen wasn't wearing any rubber But/ butt didn't seem to care as His back was turned to Rooster and he was playing with his cable.

Strong safe sex theme in the Los Angeles Times compelling a bloody Rooster to read in order to find out how to get AIDS. First-aid. Band-Aids. Etc.

Los Angeles Times
CIRCULATION: 1,242,864 daily/1,576,425 Sunday
THURSDAY, MAY 23, 1991, 204 pages
DAILY 25¢ (Designated Areas Higher)

Rooster thought about what-might-have-been:

Girl, 2 ½, Stabbed to Death; Man Killed
A 2 ½-year-old girl was stabbed to death and her mother was seriously injured Monday night. Police said a man who knew the woman was also stabbed to death in the incident at an apartment building on Alameda Street, Compton. The names of all three were withheld pending notification of family members. According to police, the man entered the woman's apartment to use her phone, but drew a knife and attacked her. All three were stabbed during the struggle. "He just accosted her for reasons that are unclear," Sgt. Brad Bennett said. "He was an acquaintance of the woman. The accosting may have been of a sexual nature."

"The newspapers reported an inaccuracy," Rooster said. "The murder weapon was a nigger flicker." Rooster smeared blood all over his face and hands, his big head wobbling like a dented globe set with millions of people. Half-dossing in a blue funk, he thought about his daddy, the menace of the nigger flicker. Rooster sweated blood. He saw a long line of violence Little Black Man and The Devil. Like father Like son Like hell.

Imagine being stabbed by your own nigger flicker. Fun? Impossible? Bizarre? Asinine? Rooster cracked up.

He was livin' large Gaudy Gold chains linking/tangling swinging around his neck like rope touching silver on the sidewalk No Copper.

Suspect in 10 Rapes Arrested After Chase
By DAVID FREED, Times Staff Writer
A 24-year-old man suspected in a string of at least 10 rapes in three cities was arrested early Tues-

day after running from a residence in southwest
Los Angeles and leading police on a brief car
chase, authorities, said.

Yolanda looked disgusted/frustrated regretting this day fighting back the tears beating the rocks thinking wondering hoping
that Billy Bugle Boy has disguised himself as one of the repairmen
Mr. Fix-it Handy Man. The aftermath Terrible storm. Lights out &
a lover to turn her on.

Rooster laughed under the tree, his eyes shaded, his face ajar,
his mouth chewing gum, dinosaur teeth acting playful. Stealing
looks Rooster the robber Rooster a thief gaining insidiously Sitting
deviously in the dark showing his horns. Bleeding Grinning
Tripping. She would probably throw up at the sight Squeamish
weak battered bruised Feeling the funk left by the Boogie-man but
Seemingly Sensing the mimicry of a Devil.

Rooster planned to get her and then end it all. He knew how
to get away with murder, now that Billy Bugle Boy was gone.

Shots Fired at Set of Gang Film; 1 Hurt

By STEPHEN BRAUN, Times Staff Writer
A movie company completing a film on gang life
in the El Sereno area of Los Angeles got a taste
of the real thing early Saturday when shots were
fired at the set during a drive-by incident, injuring
an actor, police said.

Police were unsure of a motive.

"It could have been anything," Sgt. Robert
Gruszecky said. "There were some officers there.
Maybe they were the targets. One of our big
concerns was the number of actors roaming
around the area dressed up in gang clothes. It
could have been that, or any of 100 different
reasons."

Rooster could do anything. Be anything. Fuck anything. The drugs were a cop-out an excuse a license to ill a Spike Lee joint a trip a Kool breeze a mulatto heroine bitch like Yolanda a bomb in Bob Marley's mouth a fix a drive to Colorado (Suicide) Bridge in Pasadena a quake a fallout a clod of blue grass a firebug a sucker MC a freak out a bag of candy a house party a red Devil. LOS ANGELES COUNTY—Rooster California dreamin'. Shit happens. Old wounds never heal. Blood is thicker than tequila, Rooster attested. Rooster as weak as water. High as a kite. Ego-trippin'. Stabbed by a nigger flicker sharp as a tack. In the prime of his life. A squirrel trying to get a nut. Thought he had nothing to lose but was dead wrong. Problem child. Being Black his whole life's story. A victim of circumstance. They all look alike anyway, packed like sardines in the same boat. Poor and disadvantaged. No excuse. No offense. But, poor and disadvantaged. Eventually, they got on each other's nerves. Starting dogging each other out. Finally, Rooster got sick and tired of the ain't-yo'momma-on-the-back-of-the-pancake-box jokes.

That's just my theory.

Community Caught in Back-and-forth Battle
By PAUL SMITH, Staff Writer

LA PUENTE—There's good news and bad news in one statistical trend reported from the notorious Laura and Valley area where flagrant rock cocaine dealing is an everyday fact of life, authorities said.

The good news is that narcotics arrests in the area fell 27 percent from 1989's total of 1,015 arrests to a total of 739 arrests in 1990, according to the Sheriff's Department.

The bad news is that street dealing, virtually eliminated from the area for several months last year during intensive 24-hour-a-day sweeps by deputies in the densely populated, four square-block area, has slowly returned, said Lt. David Betkey.

Rooster used the grapevine to find Yolanda. Trash in the streets, Rooster a regular Jack traveling a beanstalk for the golden goose. Yolanda fair skin Black woman unsuspecting unwinding unreserved unmasking herself to a wayfarer, Rooster bleeding revenge. Bad blood. Rooster leaning over on his side dripping dying dyeing Muddy Waters his face changing from brown to red. Murder and rape in cold blood.

Everything premeditated Yolanda grabbing the repairman's cable wanting to do it with Billy Bugle Boy but taking anything she can get. She stopped everything too crude too cheap too easy But he kept going pulling down on her panties eating flowers begging her to give it to him.

"Quit," she said. She smacked him in the face.

"Fuckin' cunt around-the-way bitch slutty dumb-ass freak!" he called her. "Turn on yo' electricity by yourself!"

Rooster thought she'd cry like a white woman in the movies on television Liz'beth Taylor etc. but Black women don't play that shit.

"Shoot, it's obvious to me you can't turn me on," Yolanda said One Black hand on her hip the other pointing at his face Head moving up and down as she talked. "I've seen more meat on a cheese stick. Now take yo' Black ass home."

The other repairmen Clapped Laughed Patted Mr. Right on his back and they all left Cable between their legs. Yolanda Questioned the fairness of life the Reason Billy would rather fuck a white woman Why he hit her Broke her Crushed her heart Yolanda left wondering why caged birds sing.

LETTERS TO THE TIMES
Britain's Queen Elizabeth II

I couldn't help noticing the sad juxtaposition of two stories on your front page (May 15): "Queen

Eats Soul Food in Los Angeles" and "Winnie
Mandela Is Sentenced to 6 Years in Prison."
EVETTE KING
Watts

Rooster bled more freely under a tree chomping candy hard and
noisily Tuning out the world switching back and forth between
present and Past a bottle of Campho Phenique for infection
Yolanda in full view.

How to Write Us
The Times welcomes expressions of all views.

Brutal (Stabbing is)...Rooster Hurt and Hiding on Somebody's
stoop in Compton Yolanda thinking She Miss It or Miss Fine
swinging on the porch past the bars that cover her front door and
window.

Accountability in the LAPD
I agree...that we need to heal the wounds of this
city. But wounds do not heal unless they are
treated.
COUNCILMAN MICHAEL WOO
Los Angeles

Bleeding Rooster looked on with bitter repulsion sore burning
Causing him to slump over But he planned to get her and then end
it all so he made his move Crawling through the wet grass like a
snake (Yolanda swinging) Crawling through wet blades (Yolanda
swinging) Crawling and hurting like a snail coming out of salt
(Yolanda swinging) Creeping up to her side Grabbing her leg
Dragging her down to the ground Throwing blood up against her
Yolanda screamed.

Tussle. Street fight. All-star wrestling. Rooster licking the
flowers wanting a virgin like father Like son. He pulled down

Yolanda's panties slid on top of her making sure she could feel it Stinging Burning She screamed.
"Quit!" she yelled. "Stop!"
Nobody could hear The neighbors in Compton blasting Loud music Yolanda squeezing the tracks in Rooster's arms.

Gang Life Contains Short Life Span
By CINDY RANSOM, Times Staff Writer
As a teenager growing up in a San Pedro housing project, Lionel "Little Train" Taylor thought being a gang member was cool—until he and his friend, Leon Jackson, were fatally shot as they climbed the stairs to crash a house party.

Yolanda screaming. "Please stop! Oh God!"
Rooster threw her dress into a T-shirt Feeling the climax Coming Yolanda wiggling underneath him screwing herself hitting the steps.
Oh God a terrible headache Yolanda's screaming reminding Rooster of the little children running around at The Swap Meet on Manchester South Central Los Angeles:
"You like?" an oriental woman in the booth asked Rooster, showing him a By Any Means Necessary T-shirt.
"Hey, if you don't stop running I'm going to bust you in the mouth!" a Black woman cried.
"You like?" asked the Chink, holding up a shirt of Bay-Bay's kids. "Only three for ten dollar."
"Stop it!"
"How about this?" she asked.
"What is it?" asked Rooster.
"Get over here before I whip yo' ass!"
"From the movie," the oriental woman answered.
"Get yo' fingers off of that!"
"How much is it?" Rooster asked.
"Alright, don't make me get up!"

"3.50 apiece."

"Leave that man alone before he goes off!"

"$3," said Rooster.

"Three for 10 dollar," said the woman.

"Sit yo' little ass down!"

"How much for one?" asked Rooster.

"Did you hear me?"

"3.50."

"I said sit yo' little ass down!"

"Look how much I've spent!" shouted Rooster.

"Quit showing out!"

"Free pair of sock," said the woman.

"Free shirt," demanded Rooster.

"What's yo' damn problem?"

"OK, three dollar."

"Give me extra-large," demanded Rooster.

"No extra-large," she said.

"You want yo' daddy to come beat yo' ass?"

"Shut up!" Rooster shouted Dripping a Stream of Consciousness Yolanda stained with Blood.

"Get off me!" cried Yolanda. "You through!"

"Goodnight," said Rooster. "You about to be dusted. I'm the sandman."

He cackled like it was nothing Lying in the grass.

Straight Outta Compton

"WHAT FOOL HATH added water to the sea, or brought a faggot to bright-burning Troy?" Clive asked. He was quoting Titus Andronicus.

She was a proud Afro-American woman, but things were falling apart in Compton, including her. Black men were disappearing all over, and she just couldn't handle it.

"Get away from me," she said.

He asked her what the distance was between two points if the first one was located in the middle of an imperfect circle and the second point marked the end of a long, straight line.

He was tripping, she thought. He had many too many toothpicks in his damn mouth.

She answered him, but not before she told him how nosey his black ass was.

"Just answer the fucking question," he said.

She got all ugly and started twisting and turning and shaking her big head.

"Fuck you," she said.

He smacked himself on the head. He had been wanting it forever.

Once, he broke down and begged her: "Please, baby, baby, please." He was quoting She's Gotta Have It.

(She glanced at a line of musicians out in the middle of the street and swore that she saw Branford Marsalis.)

"Forget it," she said. "Why would I want a nasty, irresponsible, immature, cheap, tasteless, winky-dinky dog like you?"

He shrugged his shoulders. He was trying to think if she had gotten that "winky-dinky dog" from Robert Townsend.

It threw his timing off.

"Freak," he said. Then he went home.

But he saw her the next day and asked her again. "Please, baby, baby, please." His hands and knees got black as he scooted along the dirt on the sidewalk, trailing her.

"Boy, what fuckin thing do you want?" she asked.

He lifted himself up and burst a nut in his hand.

"You ain't getting none of this," she said.

(She glanced again and saw cracked palms and ashy arms bent like elbow macaroni around a guitar, its strings glistening like long, thin blades of bluegrass in the burning sun.)

"What kind of dope are you on?" she asked.

He cracked another pecan in his moist palm.

"Do me, baby," he said. He picked it up from a song somewhere.

"Go to hell," she said.

"Hell is paved with priests' skulls," he answered.

He knew St. John Chrysostom.

"Do the right thang," she said. It sounded kind of seddity, like she was making fun of Blaxploitation films.

"The road to Hell is paved with good intentions," he said. He knew Marx, too.

She glared as he cracked another pecan in his palm. The nut exploded from inside and landed on the white cement. He threw the empty shell down and jumped and crushed it. Then he allowed his big, black fingers to drop and brush her booty.

She drew back. She had a big stereophonic booty.

"Can't touch this," she said. She had been watching M.C. Hammer on a music video, and he had turned her out.

"How come I can't have it, but Easy E and 2 Live Crew can get you all night long?" he asked.

"Cause your rap is weak," she said. She watched MTV to death.

He jingled and jangled a nickel-dime in his front pants pocket, gazed down between them, stood like a laughing hyena.

She looked the other way.

He got mad as hell.

"Just fuck it," he mumbled. He was tired of begging for it.

He peeped their concept.

She wore a faded black pair of Sassoon jeans and a black-and-white blouse that buttoned up in the back.

He wore black baggies with seven pleats and a white pleated shirt with wide sleeves that made him look like a buccaneer.

"I think we both prove that black can positive," he said. He had Spritz in his hair and blew cool mint in her face.

"You better take another look at yourself in the mirror," she said. "Vampires don't cast reflections."

He paid her no attention. "You got a big juicy butt," he said, his sleeves rolling all in the wind like sails at Venice Beach.

He wondered if Gore Vidal would be talking to her like this.

They saw a jitterbug tap on a wooden crate, an empty Coke can in the short grass, pennies and dimes dropping like water, the man looking down at his shoes—biscuit toes, wing-tips, scraped bottoms, glossy patent leather, cracked black skin, Charlie Parker on dude-man's mind as he did his own thing to well-timed claps.

Clive snapped his fingers.

A man from West Indies crept up and shouted. "Sandy, give me some of that Jamaica funk!" he screamed.

She and Clive traded trips.

"Everything is getting out of control," said Clive.

"Ah yes!" screamed the man. He leaned over and made a personal statement to Clive. "These are people who'd rather die being themselves than be on Arsenio Hall."

Clive turned and stared. "Who are you?" he asked.

The man shook the dreadlocks away from his eyes. "Can't

ya' tell man?"

"Not with that braided hair and shit dangling in your face," Clive answered.

The man grabbed onto a lock of hair. "This means that I'm cool, ethnic, Kool, and that I won't get a fuckin job in this country."

"You jumped on the bandwagon," Clive said.

"Right now, ethnicity is what's happening," said the man.

"Yes, but never dance to the beat of a different drummer," Clive said.

"Speak for yourself," said the man.

"That's the right idea," said Clive, but the man picked up his bag and walked away, refusing to listen.

"What's his problem?" she asked.

"He's got a hardhead," Clive answered.

"Yes, but why—tell me why," she demanded.

"Because he's tangled up in something he can't get out of," Clive said.

"What?" she asked.

"Beats me," Clive answered.

Clive spaced out and then came back. "Where were we?" he asked.

She said nothing.

"Don't diss me," said Clive, pointing his finger in her face.

Clive kept getting pieces of shell caught up on his clothes, and it was starting to bother him. He kicked out frantically, causing his zipper to fly open.

"Caca," he said. It was a Freudian thang.

"Olcum," she replied. She didn't know why she said it.

He leaned up against a pink wall and shelved himself among the brick building blocks marred by graffiti.

"You look pretty in pink," she said. She was thinking Pink Floyd.

"Yes, isn't it pretty to think so?" he replied. He was thinking Pretty Boy Floyd.

"Move the crowd," she said. "Shoo, scat, go, get out of here!"

She turned away. She couldn't believe that he had the nerve to go off.

He paid her no attention momentarily. He looked off the wall. "The Bloods are coming" was painted in red above his head. The statement was encased by a shape that was painted to look like white America.

"Godfather crips" was done in calligraphy, in black ink, below Clive's right knee.

"I'm going to get the hell out of here," he said.

"Out of where?" she asked whimsically, reaching out to him, albeit blindly.

"Out of Compton, out of nowhere, out of nothing," he answered.

She liked what he was saying, but only because it sounded like something she had read or seen on TV before.

"Don't tell what you're going to do," she said. "Just do it."

He replied: "Oh Mary Mack, Mack, Mack, all dressed in black; you got silver buttons, buttons, buttons, all down your back; said you found another love, love, love, instead of me; tell you what I'm gonna do, do, do; I'm gonna set you free."

She felt like Peppermint Patti. He pissed her off. "Don't call me Mary Mack," she said.

"You are a prima donna," he answered. He was talking rhetoric; it comes a dime a dozen.

"When the stars refuse to give light," she said, intentionally failing to finish her statement. She was throwing out jargon.

"Stella!" he said to himself. "She must be dreaming."

(He saw himself running down through the cinders of an alley, his legs hot and peppered with ashes. The night was black as a funeral; a tuxedo covered the moon. And Billy was chasing his dark ass, coming closer, ready to beat the hell out of him. "Shoot for the moon, and nothing will stop you," his daddy used to say. So he flew past a couple of stray cats and sprinted toward the general direction of the moon. He knew that he was in trouble. He was hanging on to the tails of night by a single thread.)

"I wish somebody would cut your dick off," she said. "Then maybe you would quit trippin'."

"What?" he asked.

"I said get a life, Negro."

He was tempted to give her the finger, the whole nine.

"You're running a crash course," she said, "and you're too dumb to realize it."

Clive grabbed his black thang like it was a pencil. "The system is failing me," he said.

Her words were ringing his head, ringing true, ringing with laughter—a key ring dropped inside his brain.

"Jiggle it, baby," she said, mocking him.

Her words were ringing inside his big head. "You're running a crash course," she said, "and you're too dumb to realize it."

Clive spat on the wall. He wondered what his friends in Compton would think about a hooker saying that.

"A man would have to be desperate to listen to a whore like you," Clive said.

"The mass of men lead lives of quiet desperation," she said.

("Do B.B. King!" some Negroes shouted.)

Clive heard small coins go do-flippy inside this smashed up Coke can and wondered why people would pay for blues.

Clive put a bomb in his mouth and lit it.

Rooster liked to have had a baby.

"You gone kill yourself!" he shouted.

"Jiggle it, baby," she said.

Clive wouldn't do it.

She snatched the bomb from Clive and blew in Rooster's face like it was nothing.

"Do me," said Rooster, eyeing the joint in her mouth.

"You the nastiest motherfucker I know," she said.

A ring of truth. That statement, made years ago, turned out to be a ring of truth.

"Pull yourself together, man," she said.

He snapped out of it.

"You talking out the side of your neck," she informed him.

"Cheap, low-down, dirty bitch," he thought. "Who was she to talk?"

He hit on her two times:

1. Treat her like a prostitute.
2. Treat her like a lady.

"I love you," Clive told her. "I want to give you everything I've got."

His statement made her stop shaking her big head and pause.

"You mean it?" she asked.

"I'm a good guy, and I'll be your friend till the end," he said. He stole the line from *Child's Play*, a horror movie on cable television.

"You so sweet," she replied.

"I'm just being myself," he said. He was dialogin' her, and now he realized that it was starting to work.

He flipped her a Charm's sour cherry sucker as she looked him over. She did need some—sex, that is—but she couldn't stop wondering if she had used too much Opium. She didn't like to smell of too much perfume. She didn't need a big penis; it would make her too sore, and she was sore already. She shouldn't have put on so much Opium, she thought. She saw him take a step backward.

With his big black hands, he pretended to frame her mouth.

"Your lips would make a lollipop too happy," he said.

"Morris Day?" she asked.

"Yep," he said, though surprised that she was able to guess the quote.

He leaned forward and puckered his mouth. His mahogany-colored lips blew up, and smelled, like bologna being fried in a skillet.

"Kiss," he said.

"Um, Prince!" she shouted.

"The world is full of queers," he muttered to himself.

He went off.

"I'm not talking about that guitar-playing, ruffle shirt-wearing, doll-loving, soft-and-wet looking, purple passionate pretty-boy faggot from Minneapolis!" he screamed. "I mean give me a kiss, you stupitt bitch!"

"Fuck you," she said.

He smacked himself on the head. "What?" he asked.

"Kiss my ass," she said.

A smile broke over his lips as he pondered the suggestion. She had a big, juicy butt. He estimated she wore a size large in panties.

"Kronka," he said. It meant "let the games begin." He got it from a Star Trek movie.

"I wouldn't let you do me if you were the last man on earth," she said.

"Ah," he said. He kept smiling.

"You got a problem," she replied, gazing down at his pants.

"What?" he asked.

"You act like you big stuff," she said matter-of-factly like.

"So? What's wrong with that?"

"I don't like big men," she said. "They make me sick."

"I don't know why you don't like big men," he said. "You a big-ass woman."

She shut him out of her world like a Venetian blind.

"Just like that?" he asked.

She pulled a smoke out from her leather purse and lit it.

"You played yourself, boy," she said.

"I thought those days were gone when we would get stoned," Clive said. "You still do it?"

"Doesn't everybody in Compton?" she said.

"Why don't you get the cigarette out your mouth?" he said. "You slobberin' all over it anyway."

"Just go, Clive," she said.

"Don't you love me?" he asked.

"I don't even know who you are," she said.

"This is how you want it?" he asked. His dogs were killing him.

"Are we through?"

"Get out of my life," she said. "There ain't no happenings here."

"Just like that?" he asked. "You just gonna shit on me and toss me aside like a used Maxi Pad, huh?"

She shook her big head, Yes.

"Just go home, Clive," she said. "Go back to your nappy-head girlfriend, your momma and all that other shit you left behind. Go back to baseball, hot dogs, apple pie and that ugly-ass pink Chevrolet that you tried to make look like a Cadillac with your dumb-ass self."

"You don't know what you're talking about," he said.

She was acting kind of funny in his opinion, like she had been playing round with a Ouija board or something.

"There must be another man tapping the boody," he thought. "Why else would she be acting so stupid?"

"You a no-good cheatin' bitch," he told her. "You got no soul."

"Maybe so, but it's over between you and me, nigger," she replied.

He walked off, sort of. "So let it be written, so let it be done," he said.

Then, with his middle finger, he drew up a lesson to remember about Compton: "You got to first be in it before you can get out of it."

"I hope you slip and fall over a crack in the sidewalk," she said from the back of his foot. "Then try to be Pharoah."

And so it goes.

He was in the mood for bullshit, so he repeated the question. The one that she left unanswered, I mean.

"What's your problem?" she asked. "How come you won't leave me alone?"

"How come you're dating a white man?" he asked.

"Why you care why?" she wondered. She leaned up against the stop sign, then spat the question out to him.

"Cause I just do," he said.

She was slightly puzzled but annoyed and didn't want to take the time to figure him out.

"Fuck you," she said. Then she paused.

"Have I said that already?" she asked.

He drew up a mental picture:

Difficult geometric calculations + Circle.

"We're getting nowhere," he said to himself. "Déjà Vu." He was quoting from "The Best of Dion Warwick" album. His momma said it was soothing. But that's another story and should be told later.

"You be fly," he said. He became the blade runner.

"Where you going?" she hollered.

"No place you'd be interested in," he shouted. He saw a speed bump on the pavement as he sprinted toward his car, and shortly afterwards there was a knock-knock sound followed by an "aw" and a thud.

"I know you shame, honey," said a woman's voice from along the sidewalk.

"Hey nigger, you must got the Holy Ghost in you," a man shouted.

"I bet your insurance won't even cover this," said a second man.

"Shit," said Clive, getting up to wipe his elbows as they bled and hollered shit while dirt fell off.

"Say man, you got a buck that I can borrow just until I get down the street?" asked a boy.

"I don't believe this," Clive said.

"Just until I get down the street, man," said the boy.

"If I were you, I'd go home," said the woman.

"You must have seen the burning bush."

"Damn, homeboy—you do have insurance, don't you?"

"How did it happen?" someone asked.

"Yo, check this out: Homeboy was running down the street and then he just fell and fucked himself up."

"Who fell?"

"Him."

"Are you serious?"

"If I'm lying, I hope I get hit by a garbage truck."

"What happened?"

"Homeboy was running down the street trying to get away from an orange truck and then he just fell and fucked himself up."

"No kidding?"

"If I'm lying, I hope a garbage truck hits my black ass."

"Brother, how much do you pay for your insurance?"

"Your momma is goin' whip your ass when she sees you."

"Who going to get their ass beat?"

"That brother over there."

"Why? What did he do?"

"Homeboy was running down the street after robbing a liquor store and then he just fell and fucked himself up."

"That's unreal."

"If I'm lying, may a garbage truck run over my ass."

"What's all this noise about?"

"Homeboy over there was running from the police and then he just fell and fucked himself up."

"I am the police."

"Well, shit, what you asking me questions for?"

"I hope the brother got a two-hundred-dollar deductible."

"I'd like to know why his momma ain't out here."

"We don't need the fuzz, man."

"It wasn't that deep."

"Go on, with yo' bad self."

"Yeah, slide on."

"Hasta la vista, baby."

"Yo man, you going to give me my buck or what?"

"Say brother, you from the Farm?"

"You had no business out in the street anyway?"

"You fucked yourself up good, homeboy."

"Get Met. It pays."

Clive dusted his clothes, grass and shit in his hair. He wiped his hands clean of pebbles. He saw them vibrate on the cement.

"FM 92, The Beat!"

"What is that?" Clive asked.

"A boomin' system," said somebody.

"I hope the brother got earthquake insurance."

"His momma ought to lock him up."

"He must be making cash money."

"It's L.L. Kool Joint!" someone shouted.

"He's a one-man gang!"

"A dope addict."

"A drug lord."

"A Saint."

"What he needs is a momma to whup his ass."

"A good policy."

"Some homeboys to chill out with."

"Somebody needs to slap the shit out of him."

"Sell him bad health insurance."

"Exploit homey, turn him into a clown and let him die."

"Take his last dollar away from him."

"Shut up!" Clive said. "I hear him. He sounds like a radio made in Japan."

"Bass. B-b-bass. Bass, bass, bass. With music by our side to break the color lines, let's work together to improve our way of life...."

"I know that pavement tore your ass up, didn't it?"

"Say man, if you ain't got a dollar, just give me fifty cents den."

People of the world today, are we looking for a better way of life. Sing! We are apart of the rhythm nation...."

"Damn, homey, you was lucky as hell. You almost swallowed those toothpicks in your mouth."

"Give me a quarter, man. I ain't playing. I gotta go!"

"That was Janet Jackson. And you're in the mix on Power 106...Power 106...Power 106...."

L.L. Kool Joint stepped up and blew marijuana in Clive's face. The music dragged temporarily, forcing him to bang on the box.

"Fuck these batteries," he said.

"Get your funk out of my face," Clive said.

"In case you haven't noticed, I'm L.L. Kool Joint."

The music whined some more.

"Welcome to the terror dome...Boy-y-y-y-y!"

"Public Enemy!" people shouted. "Let's move the crowd!" Everyone cleared out, except Clive.

"Boo!" yelled L.L. Kool Joint. "Move the crowd!"

"What's the L.K.L. on your medallion stand for?" asked Clive.

L.L. Kool J stuck out his chest and grabbed the leather medallion. "Larry King [if he was] Live [cool]," he said.

"So what's on your mind?" Clive asked.

L.L. twisted the black knob on his box and turned it off.

"Hats," he said. "Take that funky gold off your neck and put on a L.L. Kool J hat before I strike like a panther."

"What's your problem?" Clive asked.

"When in Rome, you do as the Romans do," the brother demanded.

"Where did that quote come from?" Clive asked.

"All of my lines are fresh," said L.L.

"Don't believe the hype," said Clive. He was quoting Public Enemy. That made the dude mad.

"Man, I don't know who you are, but if you don't get out of my face and out of my territory, I'm gonna kick your ass," he said. "You know what that is?"

"You'd better get with the program. I just might kick your ass anyway because I really don't like your attitude. You know what I'm saying?"

"Yeah, I know what you're saying," answered Clive.

"Then shut the fuck up then," the dude demanded. He hit Clive over the back with his box and broke it; pieces of black plastic flipped into the air like little daggers stabbing mother nature.

"I could fuck you up right now but I'm gonna give you something that I didn't have," said L.L. Kool J. (He liked cliches.)

"Besides," L.L. added, "there's word on the street of a motherfucker at-large. Considering the way you dissed Rooster, I'd go home and check my momma if I were you. You know what I'm saying?"

L.L. cracked up.

"I never dissed Rooster!" Clive shouted.

"Yes, but he thinks that you did," laughed L.L. "According to the grapevine, he's looking for you. When he finds you...." L.L. slid his fingers across his throat.

"Damn!" cried Clive. Then he took off running clean down the middle of the street, leaving his left shoe behind where he tripped.

"Never leave a brother hanging," said L.L. Kool Joint. He chuckled a little bit more in the shadow of a palm tree. Then he went to sleep.

Meantime, back at the stop sign:

"I hope 'bright-burning Troy' is not caught up in that gang shit again," she said aloud to herself, worried about Clive. A little spit came out of her mouth, but the wind threw it back in her face.

Clive stopped running to check his elbows in the back of an alley. They were stinging like hell, skin hanging and looking like gingersnaps. Clive tore the skin off and then raised his big head and grimaced.

"Aw-w-w-w-w-w-w!" he screamed. He was glad that Rooster-nem weren't around because they would have called him a sissy. But this was men shit, men's business, and Rooster-nem could now understand the pain that he had been going through.

"Sometimes a man has gotta do what a man has gotta do," Clive said to himself. He ripped two pieces of cloth from his shirt and tied them around his elbows.

He looked all around for his car: "Come to Daddy," he said. It was a significant quote, but he didn't know why.

Clive saw a man in the alley that reminded him of Bosco. He wore corduroy pants and carried a big cardboard box in his hands. The box was the size of a stove.

"He need to comb his head," Clive said. "Out of a slew of homeless people, why him?"

The man paid Clive no attention. He threw the box down, climbed over the top and got inside. Clive watched him unzip his pants and urinate.

"Ugh-h-h," Clive muttered to himself. There was a dent in his forehead when he said it. The man got out of the box, picked it back up and zigzagged away.

"I see you just gonna go ahead and take the shit with you," Clive said very softly. "That's cool. Cause I don't want to step in the mess anyway."

Clive finally spotted his car. He could see that the thing was where it was supposed to be, and the rims were still on it, but the word "saint" had been spray-painted blue on his car door.

Clive cried. The car was his baby.

Clive opened the door and got in. The leather squealed as his butt dropped onto the seat.

"Shut up," he said.

There had been rain. No, someone had sprung a leak inside his car.

Clive pulled a faded gold key the color of his skin out of his pants pocket and stuck it into the ignition. With his black hand on the key, he twisted his wrist and, for a moment, considered slicing it. The always-hesitant car murmured.

"We should take a minute to just sit and think for a second," it said. "Now while it's clear that I don't like to get pissed on, I don't feel that this is worth me going out and getting myself all bent out of shape over."

The car squatted on its soles. "Don't do it," it said.

"Start, you son-of-a-bitch!" said Clive. Running, he meant.

Clive violently mashed down on the accelerator petal with his right shoe. His black patent leather loafer wrinkled and then looked up at him as if to say "stop, goddammit!"

The car screamed, and then it finally started up. First, it roared, and then it started spitting and squealing and screaming like a hurt nigger.

"Now wait a minute!" it said. "There's no need for blood! I got a sweet body and a leather hide, and you got on a white shirt!"

"This car makes too much noise," Clive said. He reached over and turned on the radio.

"Zzzz-cu-cu-shee-zz-ft!...Iss is Power 106, and we're jamming with 13 continuous songs! Up next—Where will you go? *on Saturday night slow jams, where music is Powr-r-r-!...Hello, caller No. 94, you're on the air. Where you calling from?...Los Angeles...What's your name...Diana Warfield...Diana, are you ready for this?...I hope so...Diana, how many songs in a row did we play?"*

"Say five!" Clive said. "They always play five!"

"Oh my gosh! Um, let's see...."

"Five!" screamed Clive.

"Uh. Oh God!..."

"Five!" shouted Clive. "Say five, you stupid bitch!"

"How many Diana?..."

"Five!" yelled Clive.

"Four?..."

"I don't believe this!" Clive shouted. "You blew it!"

"Diana...Yes?...Are you here?...Yes...Diana...You just won yourself four hundred dollars!...Oh, my God! I can't believe it!...Diana, what are you gonna do with it?...Um, well, I need a break so I'll probably take a vacation and get away from Los Angeles...Where will you go, Diana?...Maybe Virginia Beach...And do what?...Check out the men!"

She laughs.

"This is unbelievable," said Clive.

"Diana, tell everyone out there who made it all possible!...Power 106!...Here's to Virginia Beach, it's Where Will You Go? *by Babyface."*

Clive edged up the volume.

"We started out as simple friends...That kind of friends should never end."

Clive thought about his relationships with women and the days when he held Rooster on the stoop.

"But we were fortunate to care enough... We knew just where we stood...But soon as love appeared, you turned away...And you were so unsure, and so afraid, of feeling what I was feeling...You

were scared that love would blow your heart away…And you were
certain that in time our love would stray…So where will you go?
And who's gonna love you like I do?"

Clive used his wipers to clear the water off the window while
he drove. He did 85 m.p.h. on the freeway. He slammed his fist
against the dashboard.

He went off.

He took the 110 to Lynwood, smashing ev'ry fuckin' bit of the
radio with his fist.

He went off, blood trickling down his hand.

"Campho Penique!" Rooster said.

"Petroleum jelly!" shouted Clive.

"If you don't want infection, you gonna have to use Campho
Penique!" said Rooster.

Clive went off.

He took the 110 to Watts, weaving his pink car in and out the
lanes like a man trying to kill himself.

He went off.

"You get out of here!" his daddy yelled. "You ain't nothin' but
a whore!" He picked up a green mixing bowl and threw it at her.

Caddy got up and looked at Clive. Her face was smeared with
rouge where she had been hit.

"Bye, Clive," she whispered. Then she flew out the door, Heavy
D. singing Sister, Sister *on the radio.*

He went off.

He took the 110 to Graham.

Rooster gave her the finger.

Clive chuckled. "You got the wrong attitude," he said.

"What would you do if your feet were killing you and somebody
walked by cracking jokes?" asked Rooster.

Clive slapped Rooster on the foot. "Quit," he said.

He went off.

Circles. He did circles on the freeway. He was back in South
Central Los Angeles.

"…with a Bloody Mary in your hands," she said, "you left in

*such a violent and drunken state that you failed to heed the
warnings. You thought the ringing of bells in your ears were sirens,
so you walked out of my apartment shouting 'give me liberty or give
me death' and lost yourself after the storm had grew worse."*

*"Yes, this has happened to me several times," Clive continued,
"but I keep coming back because God has blessed me with nine
lives, which surely He would not have done were it not for the fact
that we were meant to be together."*

Clive stopped the car in front of his apartment building. He had
peed in his pants, so, for a moment, he sat in the car watching
children double-dutch on the sidewalk. The only boy in the group
was trying to jump the rope, but the long and heavy cord wrapped
around his neck. Clive got out of the car, untangled the rope and
gave the boy a dollar with blue ink on the paper and funk for a
number.

He gazed inside and saw the television on in his momma's
bedroom.

"So many one-ways in LA," Clive said. He had been through so
many one-ways in LA

He sprinted to the door and strolled in, the television blasting,
his momma out on the sofa.

"...In the news today, an unidentified man was hit by a garbage
truck in Compton. This, and more news, coming up after the
Lakers' game..."

She woke up and slapped his big head with a shoe.

"Get out of here!" she shouted. "You grown now."

Clive looked at his momma like what's-up. "I was going
anyway," he said.

She pulled out the photo album.

"I remember when you was born," she said. "You was a fat
baby. You weighed eight pounds and eleven ounces. You was on
milk and cereal almost by the time we took you out of the
hospital...."

Clive stood and looked like oh-brother.

"Momma," he said.

"Back then, you were easy to take care of. You never complained. You were satisfied with a bottle of formula. You were born with your eyes closed...."

"Momma!" shouted Clive.

"Don't interrupt your momma!" she shouted.

"Momma, I gotta go!"

"Just don't forget where you came from," she said.

Clive opened the door and walked out. "I'm straight outta Compton!" he yelled.

RECENT TITLES FROM FC2

From the District File
A novel by Kenneth Bernard
From the District File depicts a bureaucratic world of supercontrolled
oppressiveness in the not-too-distant future. *Publishers Weekly*
calls Bernard's fiction "a confrontation with the inexpressible...a
provocative comment on the restrictiveness and pretension of our
lives."
128 pages, Cloth: $18.95, Paper: $8.95

Double or Nothing
A novel by Raymond Federman
"Invention of this quality ranks the book among the fictional
masterpieces of our age...I have read *Double or Nothing* several
times and am not finished with it yet, for it is filled with the kinds
of allusion and complexity that scholars will feast upon for years.
Were literature a stock market, I'd invest in this book—Richard
Kostelanetz
320 pages, Paper: $10.95

F/32
A novel by Eurudice
F/32 is a wild, eccentric, Rabaelaisian romp through most forms
of amorous excess. But, it is also a troubling tale orbiting around
a public sexual assault on the streets of Manhattan. Between the
poles of desire and butchery, the novel and Ela sail, the awed
reader going along for one of the most dazzling rides in recent
American fiction.
250 pages, Cloth: $18.95, Paper, $8.95

Trigger Dance
Stories by Diane Glancy

"Diane Glancy writes with poetic knowledge of Native Americans...The characters of *Trigger Dance* do an intricate dance that forms wonderful new story patterns. With musical language, Diane Glancy teaches us to hear ancient American refrains amidst familiar American sounds. A beautiful book."— Maxine Hong Kingston

250 pages, Cloth: $18.95, Paper: $8.95

Is It Sexual Harassment Yet?
Stories by Cris Mazza

"The stories...continually surprise, delight, disturb, and amuse. Mazza's 'realism' captures the eerie surrealism of violence and repressed sexuality in her characters' lives."—Larry McCaffery

150 pages, Cloth: $18.95, Paper: 8.95

Napoleon's Mare
A novella by Lou Robinson

Napoleon's Mare, thirteen chapters and a section of prose poems is a diatribe, a discontinuous narrative—as much about writing as about the bewildering process of constructing a self.

186 pages, Cloth: $18.95, Paper: $8.95

Valentino's Hair
A novel by Yvonne Sapia

"Intense and magical, *Valentino's Hair* vividly creates an America intoxicated by love and death. Sapia brilliantly renders the vitality and tensions in the Puerto Rican community in 1920s New York City."—Jerome Stern. Picked as one of the top 25 books for 1991 by Publishers Weekly.

162 pages, Cloth: $18.95, Paper: $8.95

Mermaids for Attila
Stories by Jacques Servin
Mermaids for Attila is a fun, hands-on, toy-like book on the subject of well-orchestrated national behaviors. In it Servin considers the biggest horrors and the weirdest political truths. "At a time when conventional narrative fiction is making an utterly boring comeback, it is a relief to find writers like Jacques Servin who are willing to acknowledge that verbal representation can no longer be regarded as anything more than a point of departure."— Stephen-Paul Martin
128 pages, Cloth: $18.95, Paper: $8.95

Hearsay
A novel by Peter Spielberg
Hearsay is a darkly comic account of the misadventures of one Lemuel Grosz from youthbed to deathbed. In its blending of reality and irreality, *Hearsay* present a life the way we winess the life of another: from a certain distance, catching a glimpse here, a revelation there.
275 pages, Cloth: $18.95, Paper: $8.95

Close Your Eyes and Think of Dublin: Portrait of a Girl
A novel by Kathryn Thompson
A brilliant Joycean hallucination of a book in which the richness of Leopold Bloom's inner life is found in a young American girl experiencing most of the things that vexed James Joyce: sex, church, and oppression.
197 pages, Cloth: $18.95, Paper: $8.95

Books may be ordered through the Talman Company, 150 Fifth Avenue, New York, NY 10011.

For a catalog listing all books published by Fiction Collective, write to Fiction Collective Two, Department of English, Illinois State University, Normal, IL 61761-6901.